Halfhyde
on Zanatu

Historical Fiction Published by McBooks Press

ALEXANDER KENT
Midshipman Bolitho
Stand Into Danger
In Gallant Company
Sloop of War
To Glory We Steer
Command a King's Ship
Passage to Mutiny
With All Despatch
Form Line of Battle!
Enemy in Sight!
The Flag Captain
Signal–Close Action!
The Inshore Squadron
A Tradition of Victory
Success to the Brave
Colours Aloft!
Honour This Day
The Only Victor
Beyond the Reef
The Darkening Sea
For My Country's Freedom
Cross of St George
Sword of Honour
Second to None
Relentless Pursuit
Man of War

DOUGLAS REEMAN
Badge of Glory
First to Land
The Horizon
Dust on the Sea
Knife Edge

Twelve Seconds to Live
Battlecruiser
The White Guns
A Prayer for the Ship
For Valour

DAVID DONACHIE
The Devil's Own Luck
The Dying Trade
A Hanging Matter
An Element of Chance
The Scent of Betrayal
A Game of Bones

On a Making Tide
Tested by Fate
Breaking the Line

DUDLEY POPE
Ramage
Ramage & The Drumbeat
Ramage & The Freebooters
Governor Ramage R.N.
Ramage's Prize
Ramage & The Guillotine
Ramage's Diamond
Ramage's Mutiny
Ramage & The Rebels
The Ramage Touch
Ramage's Signal
Ramage & The Renegades
Ramage's Devil
Ramage's Trial
Ramage's Challenge
Ramage at Trafalgar
Ramage & The Saracens
Ramage & The Dido

ALEXANDER FULLERTON
Storm Force to Narvik
Last Lift from Crete
All the Drowning Seas

JAMES L. NELSON
The Only Life That Mattered

PHILIP MCCUTCHAN
Halfhyde at the Bight of Benin
Halfhyde's Island
Halfhyde and the
    Guns of Arrest
Halfhyde to the Narrows
Halfhyde for the Queen
Halfhyde Ordered South
Halfhyde on Zanatu

V.A. STUART
Victors and Lords
The Sepoy Mutiny
Massacre at Cawnpore
The Cannons of Lucknow
The Heroic Garrison

The Valiant Sailors
The Brave Captains
Hazard's Command
Hazard of Huntress
Hazard in Circassia
Victory at Sebastopol
Guns to the Far East
Escape from Hell

R.F. DELDERFIELD
Too Few for Drums
Seven Men of Gascony

DEWEY LAMBDIN
The French Admiral
Jester's Fortune

C.N. PARKINSON
The Guernseyman
Devil to Pay
The Fireship
Touch and Go
So Near So Far
Dead Reckoning

The Life and Times of
    Horatio Hornblower

JAN NEEDLE
A Fine Boy for Killing
The Wicked Trade
The Spithead Nymph

IRV C. ROGERS
Motoo Eetee

NICHOLAS NICASTRO
The Eighteenth Captain
Between Two Fires

FREDERICK MARRYAT
Frank Mildmay OR
    The Naval Officer
The King's Own
Mr Midshipman Easy
Newton Forster OR
    The Merchant Service
Snarleyyow OR
    The Dog Fiend
The Privateersman
The Phantom Ship

W. CLARK RUSSELL
Wreck of the Grosvenor
Yarn of Old Harbour Town

RAFAEL SABATINI
Captain Blood

MICHAEL SCOTT
Tom Cringle's Log

A.D. HOWDEN SMITH
Porto Bello Gold

The Halfhyde Adventures, No. 7

Halfhyde
on Zanatu

Philip McCutchan

MCBOOKS PRESS, INC.
ITHACA, NEW YORK

Published by McBooks Press, Inc. 2005
Copyright © 1982 by Philip McCutchan
First published in Great Britain by George Weidenfeld & Nicolson Limited

Cover painting: *British Gunboat* by Charles J. de Lacy, from *Boy's Own Paper,*
July 1911. Courtesy Mary Evans Picture Library.

Library of Congress Cataloging-in-Publication Data

McCutchan, Philip, 1920-
  Halfhyde on Zanatu / by Philip McCutchan.
    p. cm. — (The Halfhyde adventures ; no. 7)
  ISBN 1-59013-072-3 (pbk. : alk. paper)
  1. Halfhyde, St. Vincent (Fictitious character)—Fiction. 2. Great
Britain—History, Naval—Fiction. 3. British—Oceania—Fiction. 4.
Oceania—Fiction. I. Title.
  PR6063.A167H33 2005
  823'.914—dc22

                                                    2004026520

Distributed to the trade by National Book Network, Inc.
15200 NBN Way, Blue Ridge Summit, PA 17214
800-462-6420

Additional copies of this book may be ordered from any bookstore
or directly from McBooks Press, Inc., ID Booth Building,
520 North Meadow St., Ithaca, NY 14850. Please include $4.00 postage
and handling with mail orders. New York State residents must add
sales tax to total remittance (books & shipping). All McBooks Press
publications can also be ordered by calling toll-free
1-888-BOOKS11 (1-888-266-5711).
Please call to request a free catalog.

Visit the McBooks Press website at www.mcbooks.com.

Printed in the United States of America

9 8 7 6 5 4 3 2 1

Chapter 1

IT WAS A SPLENDID MORNING, fresh and invigorating after a night spent incognito in the roistering bars of Portsmouth town. Officers of Her Majesty's Fleet were not usually accustomed to drink beer and gin alongside men of the lower deck, but Lieutenant St Vincent Halfhyde found an occasional night in their company a more refreshing experience than listening to the often constipated expoundings of his brother officers. Last night, the fumes of liquor had been heavy, and still were, but the breeze coming off the waters of Spithead was beginning to clear them from his brain. Away to the east came the rumble of heavy gunfire from Fort Cumberland as the gunners of the Royal Marine Artillery were exercised in the laying and training of their batteries upon a target to the eastward of the Isle of Wight. Halfhyde, who had risen early, had walked from his lodgings in Victoria Road towards the sea, taking a long route to the dockyard. Small white horses sparkled around the sea forts; an inward-bound battleship turned for the buoyed channel to enter harbour, her seamen divisions fallen in fore and aft wearing their sennit hats, while a string of coloured bunting strained against the signal halliards. Halfhyde recognized her as the *Royal Sovereign*, launched in 1891 . . . a 14,000-ton ship of high freeboard, her four 13.5-inch guns in open barbettes neatly trained now to the fore-and-aft line for entering harbour. The on-shore breeze brought fitful music from the band of the Royal Marine Light Infantry, fallen in on the battleship's quarterdeck.

"A fine sight," Halfhyde said aloud.

Beside him, from close to the ground as he stood seaward of Southsea Castle, a small voice said fervently, "It is that, mister!"

Halfhyde looked down, raising his eyebrows: an urchin, barefoot and in ragged clothing, but with the young face alight. "It gladdens the heart, boy, does it not?"

The urchin nodded. "I'm goin' to go to sea, mister, if they'll have me."

"Then I wish you luck. How old are you?"

"Ten, mister, goin' on eleven." It was said with importance: eleven was a great age, much more so than ten. "Soon as I'm old enough, I'm goin' to join."

"You could do worse," Halfhyde said gravely. "What's the view of your parents, and of your schoolmasters?"

The urchin grinned. "Don't matter what they say, mister, I know what I want." He looked towards the stately battleship as it slid slowly past the beach; he was totally absorbed. Already he could see himself, as Halfhyde was aware, barefoot as now, nimbly climbing the steel ladders that networked the battleship below-decks, or swarming to the flag deck as a signal boy with a smart blue sailor's collar and bell-bottomed trousers.

After a word or two of encouragement Halfhyde turned away and walked on with a springy step. All was well with the Empire and would remain so as long as England's youth wanted to go to sea or join the army. A man could do no better . . . Halfhyde rounded the castle and strode across Southsea Common, coming eventually along Pembroke Road and then into the High Street of Old Portsmouth, passing the George Hotel where Lord Nelson had spent his last night on English soil before sailing away to Trafalgar and a glorious death. By the military barracks he turned left for Portsmouth Hard and the main gate of the dockyard, where he was approached by a constable of the Metropolitan Police, the force that had the honour of guarding the royal dockyards.

Halfhyde, who was in plain clothes, identified himself. "Lieutenant-in-command of *Seahorse* undergoing refit."

"All right, sir." The policeman saluted, and Halfhyde walked through into the sea smells of the yard, tangy and evocative of tar and rope and salt water, past the boatyard and the lofty warehouses and the *Royal Sovereign* now busily securing to the South Railway jetty. He walked on to the dry-dock where the torpedo-boat destroyer lay with her plates exposed and the dockyard mateys swarming all over her like busy flies with rivetting hammers and all manner of strange tools. Halfhyde sighed; she looked a mess, and had looked a mess for the last four months. With most of her former company split up and drafted to other ships, and with no living accommodation aboard her, she had temporarily ceased to live. As Halfhyde watched with distaste and tried to project his mind ahead to the day when she would recommission and go again to sea, his first lieutenant emerged from what looked like no more than a jagged hole in the superstructure. He had news. "There's a signal for you, sir, from the commander-in-chief." He handed a signal form to Halfhyde.

Halfhyde's eyebrows went up. "I'm required to attend upon the admiral at once, am I? I wonder what's in the wind now." He glanced down at his plain clothes. "No doubt at once means at once. Since my uniform is in my lodgings, I shall attend as I am."

Taken off by a dockyard boat to the old *Victory*, Halfhyde stepped aboard and was escorted with bent head along the timber decks, past the cannons that had roared Lord Nelson's thunder at the French and Spanish fleets, to be greeted by the flag lieutenant. The latter stared disdainfully at plain clothes that had seen better days: lieutenants without private means were among the world's poor. Halfhyde, the flag lieutenant said, would be admitted immediately to the admiral's presence; and was as good as his word. He turned away towards the great stern cabin once occupied by Nelson, and was quickly back and beckoning Halfhyde to follow. Halfhyde entered the cabin to find the admiral seated behind a desk, short, square, much whiskered, and impeccably uniformed, with a beautifully turk's-headed telescope gleaming on the polished mahogany and leather of the desk.

"Ah, Halfhyde." There was a glare. "What the devil d'you mean by this?"

"By what, sir?"

"By presenting yourself to me out of uniform, of course!"

"I apologize, sir, but fancied speed in execution of orders to be preferable to sartorial considerations."

"I think you're being impertinent, Mr Halfhyde, and not for the first time in your career. I advise you very strongly to guard your tongue, or you'll find yourself back on the half-pay list. I do not expect my commanding officers to appear on duty in the dockyard or aboard my flagship out of uniform, and the fact that your ship is refitting is no excuse, do you understand?"

"Yes, sir."

"Sit down, then."

Halfhyde lowered himself gladly enough into a chair: the *Victory's* deckheads were low enough to be torture to a tall man. Whilst the admiral pushed irritably at papers and signals on his desk, Halfhyde reflected on half-pay, an unsatisfactory state of affairs into which he had been projected in the past by his habit of not suffering gladly the peccadilloes of unintelligent senior officers; he had no wish to return to that state, or to Camden Town and the ministrations, however kindly, of the good Mrs Mavitty, his erstwhile landlady. He would watch his tongue when the admiral uttered again, which within the next minute he did.

"I consider your experience wasted, Mr Halfhyde, in standing by a ship undergoing refit—a refit that has lasted for longer than was expected. As it happens, I have been asked by the Admiralty to recommend an officer of lieutenant's rank for a special duty, and I have submitted your name."

"Thank you, sir. May I ask for what duty?"

The admiral nodded, looking keenly at Halfhyde. "You may. You are appointed lieutenant-in-command of the torpedo-boat destroyer *Talisman* with effect from noon tomorrow. You will leave port at noon the following day and your orders are to take your ship to the South Pacific by way of Singapore. It will be a long and hazardous voyage for a small vessel, as no doubt you are aware."

"Yes, sir. May I ask, why not enter the South Pacific by way of the South Atlantic and Cape Horn?"

"For a very good reason," the admiral said. "In Singapore you are to rendezvous with a squadron under Commodore Bassinghorn." Heavy eyebrows lifted. "I understand you have served under him in the past?"

"I have, sir, and with pleasure." Captain Bassinghorn, as he had then been, was a splendid seaman and a fine man, and a friendship had developed when Halfhyde had been Bassinghorn's first lieutenant in the old battleship *Viceroy* in Chinese waters, had been continued in the *Prince Consort* off South-West Africa and again—though only briefly before Halfhyde had been snatched away to serve under the extraordinary Captain

Watkiss—in the *Lord Cochrane* in the Mediterranean. "I shall be delighted to serve under him again."

"I am glad to hear it," the admiral said. Tapping his fingers on his desk, he went on, "Commodore Bassinghorn is flying his broad pennant in the first-class cruiser *Port Royal,* which is accompanied by the second-class cruiser *Plantagenet,* these two ships forming the Long Range Squadron. Upon your arrival off Singapore, Commodore Bassinghorn will pass his detailed orders, but I am able to inform you of their basis. The squadron is under Admiralty orders to steam towards the island of Zanatu. The Colonial Office is in receipt of intelligence to the effect that certain persons on the island, which is a British possession, are planning a revolt against our rule. This is to be nipped smartly in the bud."

"I see, sir. Could it not be nipped the more smartly by using ships already in Australian waters?"

"We have no ships available off the Australian colonies, Mr Halfhyde, otherwise, you may rest assured, the Admiralty would have used them without advice from you."

"Indeed, sir."

"I am delighted you agree," the admiral said with heavy sarcasm. "You will kindly proceed to hand over to your first lieutenant, who is appointed in command of *Seahorse* in your place."

On the stroke of noon next day Halfhyde arrived alongside *Talisman* in the dockyard basin. This time he was in uniform, with the two gold stripes of his rank glinting on his sleeves above the starched white shirt-cuffs. Looking down from the wall of the basin Halfhyde saw, with pleasure, that the *Talisman* looked a smart ship; he had not expected this. The admiral had made no mention of why the TBD's former commanding officer, a senior lieutenant, had needed replacement and Halfhyde, exercising unusual tact, had refrained from asking; but discreet enquiries made after leaving the admiral's presence had revealed that drink had been the cause. Drunken captains did not normally produce smart ships unless they had conscientious and loyal subordinates, and the fact spoke well for the first lieutenant. Meanwhile, there was activity below: the quartermaster and his gangway staff had sprung to attention and a moment later a lieutenant appeared on deck to salute his new captain aboard.

Halfhyde clambered down an almost vertical ladder and stepped on to the quarterdeck. "You are my first lieutenant?" he asked.

"Yes, sir. Name of Halliburton, sir."

Halfhyde nodded. "I trust we shall get on well together, Mr Halliburton. The ship is clean and that's a good start. I'd be obliged to be shown to my cabin, if you please."

"Aye, aye, sir." Halliburton turned and Halfhyde followed. Once inside his cabin, he faced his second-in-command, standing stiffly with his hands clasped behind his tall back. Halliburton looked willing but stolid, somewhat pudding-faced. "Your history, if you please, Mr Halliburton."

"Yes, sir." Halliburton gave a nervous hitch to his trousers. "*Britannia,* of course, for my cadet's time. Midshipman in the Flying Squadron under Lord Clanwilliam. Sub-Lieutenant in the flagship of the Atlantic Fleet. Appointed to this ship as a lieutenant, sir." Halliburton paused. "One year's seniority now, sir."

"Yes, I see." Halfhyde smiled and held out his hand. After that Halliburton had little more to say; he did not appear to be a man of much conversation and seemed ill-at-ease in his captain's presence. Halfhyde nodded a dismissal; and later, after meeting his other officers in the small ward-room, made an extended tour of the ship prior to moving to the anchorage.

At six bells in the forenoon watch next day Halfhyde said, "One hour to sailing, Mr Halliburton. I shall expect your reports of readiness in forty-five minutes."

"Aye, aye, sir."

The first lieutenant went about his business. The minutes ticked away to departure on her long voyage and Halfhyde's engineer, Mr Dappers, approached and saluted and reported his engines ready to proceed. Then Mr Halliburton, reporting the ship's company correct and the ship ready for sea.

"Thank you, Mr Halliburton. Pipe the hands to stations for leaving harbour." Halfhyde went forward to the navigating bridge, where the sub-lieutenant stood by the binnacle. The routine signal was made to the Queen's Harbour Master, asking formal permission to proceed; when this permission came, Halfhyde passed the order to weigh anchor. With the cable already shortened-in, the anchor was quickly hove-to the waterline and left underfoot in case of need; once outside the harbour it would be brought aboard to the cathead and secured for the long sea passage to Gibraltar, where the bunkers would be replenished to take the ship on through the Mediterranean for Port Said and the hot haul through the Suez Canal to the Red Sea. Halfhyde put his engines ahead for the harbour mouth, piping the still and coming to the salute as his ship proceeded past the flag of the commander-in-chief aboard the *Victory*. Moving onward he passed the *Royal Sovereign* at the South Railway jetty, and again saluted in respect for a post captain's commissioning pennant. The *Talisman* slid out through the narrow entrance, leaving the crusted walls of Fort Blockhouse to starboard and

the Round Tower to port, moving along the buoyed channel
until the transit bearings told Halfhyde when to make his turn
to starboard into the waters of Spithead, where a century before
England had been shaken by the mutiny of her fleet. Times had
changed since then; but a seaman's life was still a hard one and
the twelve thousand sea miles to Zanatu in a ship as small as
the *Talisman* would bring no comfort to any of her company.

Chapter 2

AFTER COALING SHIP, Gibraltar was left behind as a magnificent sunset flooded the harbour and the outer anchorage with colour. The bugles of the Royal Marine Light Infantry sounded across the bay from the quarterdecks of the Mediterranean Squadron, to be followed by the lowering of the White Ensigns. From the military barracks ashore came the sound of the bands of the regiments in garrison, stirring sounds of Empire, of Her Majesty Queen Victoria's sway over half the world. With the filthy coal-dust of the bunkering evolution swilled away by the wash-deck hoses, the *Talisman* steamed past Europa Point into the Mediterranean where the sea lay flat and the night sky was soon hung with a myriad stars. Behind the ship the wake streamed away westward, a bright green swathe of phosphorescence. In due course they left the great Malta base to starboard— another pillar of British might whose Grand Harbour held a powerful array of battleships and cruisers.

In Port Said they took more coal aboard before the passage of the canal. In Aden, and in Colombo, and once more in Singapore, *Talisman* bunkered again. On their arrival Commodore Bassinghorn was conspicuous only by his absence; and during the coaling operation a hand message was brought aboard from Government House. The Long Range Squadron had been delayed in sailing from Hong Kong, and Halfhyde was now ordered to make a rendezvous off the island of Woleai in longitude 143°

east, latitude 7° north. When the rendezvous was made, the reinforced squadron would steam direct for Zanatu at its maximum speed.

Coaling once again completed, Halfhyde took the *Talisman* out through the Singapore Strait and headed nor'-nor'-east into the South China Sea to come round the northern tip of Borneo, thence altering to the eastward through the Balabac Strait and passing between the islands of the Sulu archipelago into the Celebes Sea.

It was nearly three days later that trouble came.

As the ship left the Celebes Sea, passing between Karakelong Island and Tinaca Point at the southern tip of Mindanao, and moving into the Pacific Ocean, sliding onward through a glassy sea, Halfhyde noted a sudden and foreboding fall in the barometric pressure and sent at once for his first lieutenant.

"The glass, Mr Halliburton. It's falling fast."

"Yes, sir?"

"Yes, Mr Halliburton. And it's the month of August, is it not?"

"Yes, it is, sir." Halliburton's white uniform was stretched like a drum over his ample figure; the brass buttons appeared to be about to part company with the material.

"August is the typhoon season—and I say again, the glass is falling. Have you any experience of typhoons, by any chance?"

"No. No, I haven't, sir—"

"In that case you are about to add to your knowledge, since a typhoon is approaching. As my first lieutenant, if I need to remind you, the safety of the ship will depend largely upon your preparations. We shall take a look at the chart, Mr Halliburton, and then you will see to it that everything is securely battened down below-decks and that all upper-deck gear is double lashed. You will pay particular attention to the boats and the anchors."

Halfhyde turned to the chart-table at the after end of the bridge and with his first lieutenant put his head in through the canvas screen. Halfhyde indicated the warm equatorial Pacific to the south-east of the ship's current position, the area where the terrible typhoons originate and then extend swiftly north-westward over the Philippines towards the coast of China. Leaving the chart-table, Halfhyde walked to the fore end of the navigating bridge and looked all around the horizons.

To starboard a long, low line of thick black cloud was already forming; even as Halfhyde watched, the menacing line grew larger, fanning out towards the torpedo-boat destroyer. A wind whipped blusteringly around the vessel, cold and dismal, bringing a rapid change to the day and becoming stronger by the minute.

Halfhyde sniffed that wind, looked again at the fast-extending cloud. "Mr Halliburton," he called.

"Yes, sir?"

"We have no time to lose. We're about to be struck, and struck hard."

The pipe was for all hands; Halliburton gave his orders to the chief boatswain's mate to make all secure, and himself checked around the ship above and below. With the wind increasing the sea grew disturbed and grey, and rain began to fall. The sea-boats were griped-in hard to the davits and extra lashings passed; the anchors were double-stropped at the catheads and the cable-clenches were given another turn to prevent any movement of the heavy links along the turtle-decked fo'c'sle-head. Life-lines were rove fore and aft along the upper deck, though once the full weight of the typhoon struck, all hands would have to remain at their stations and not risk movement along the decks except in direst emergency. By the time Halliburton reported back to the captain, the wind had increased further and was howling like a mad orchestra through the rigging, and the rain was coming down in solid, soaking sheets of water.

Halfhyde had increased speed to stand clear, so far as was possible, of the storm centre; and he indicated that he had altered course a little to the north-east.

The first lieutenant shouted back, his mouth close to Halfhyde's ear. "Why's that, sir?"

"The typhoon will move north-westerly, as I have already said. Since it may well be some eighty miles in diameter we may not escape it, but I propose to try."

"Yes, sir." Halliburton hesitated, then shouted again. "What do we do now, sir?"

Halfhyde gave a cold grimace. "Pray, Mr Halliburton!"

"Pray, sir?"

"And hope. It's all we can do. And watch carefully . . . if the typhoon overtakes us we shall be in difficulties. I've no desire to be pooped by trying to run before it northwards, nor to broach-to if I maintain my present course too long. Therefore I may try to turn the ship and head her into the wind and sea, with revolutions enough to keep the ship's head steady, and wait for the storm to pass." He lifted his telescope, staring through the downpour towards the turbulence astern. By now the whole sky was overcast to the point of blackness, and the day had suddenly turned into night, a night of no stars or moon. The wind roared and shrieked and the bridge rose and fell and lurched to port and starboard as the filthy weather swept up from astern, to overtake them. Halfhyde watched in growing anxiety; within the next half-hour it became evident that they were not going to stand clear, and he moved to the engine-room voice-pipe to speak personally to the engineer.

"Mr Dappers, I intend to turn into the wind. Warn the boiler-room, if you please, and stand by for frequent alterations to the revolutions." Halfhyde snapped back the cover of the voice-pipe and grabbed for a stanchion as the deck seemed to fall away beneath his feet. "Mr Halliburton, the wheel hard-a-port!"

"Hard-a-port, sir." Halliburton passed the order to the torpedo-coxswain, who had now taken the wheel himself. Everyone on the bridge held his breath as the *Talisman,* answering her port helm, came round to starboard. There was violent movement now as a wave took her abeam and laid her over until it began to seem as though she would never stop. Ordering an increase in revolutions, Halfhyde held tight to his stanchion and looked down the ship's side as the water surged and raced a matter of inches below the bridge. He could have left it too long . . . before now, ships bigger than his had broached-to and had been lost without trace as the water thundered aboard and forced them down below the surface, helpless when the huge waves took them broadside on. From below-decks, agonizing sounds came: the crash of crockery that had burst through cupboard doors, the shift of stores and coal—a shift that could seriously affect the ship's stability and make her unmanageable even if they survived this turn into wind and sea. Halfhyde spared a thought for the toiling stokers at the open furnace mouths in the boiler-room where the red-hot coal would be flying along with that as yet unburned, and men would be sliding willy-nilly across the steel deck to fetch up with their naked skin laid across the lick of the fires themselves, or the hot iron of the doors.

Over she went, to lie like a dying duck. Her very plates seemed to groan and protest and she came no farther round as the solid water dropped aboard and the wind continued its death-like howl. Then she gave an extra lurch to port and her bows rose sharply as a vast wave slid beneath her stem. Halfhyde, flung sideways and backwards, lost his grip of the stanchion, fell heavily to the deck, and rolled beneath the guardrail towards the sea.

Halfhyde's mind was full of nightmares: the ship was sinking, was already on its way to the cluttered bottom of the eastern seas to join the pirate junks and the merchantmen and men-of-war that had come to grief over the centuries. Past memories flitted before him: once again he fought his battles with the Russian, Admiral Prince Gorsinski, one of them not so far north of this very area. He saw again the German, Admiral Paulus von Merkatz, with whom he had crossed swords in Africa and in South America. The incredible Detective Inspector Todhunter came to him with his bowler hat held across his chest and eyes downcast as he looked upon death. He saw the equally incredible Captain Watkiss, strutting pompously in his over-long white shorts, monocle dropping from his choleric eye and telescope upraised in characteristic wrath. But gradually the mists cleared and he realized that he was lying upon a bunk and that there was a safe bottom beneath although the ship was still lifting and falling to restless seas. His head ached abominably and he felt sick; and he was swathed in many bandages.

He became aware of someone sitting by the bunk, someone who got up and bent over him as his eyes were seen to be open.

"It's me, sir," the figure said, "Bodger, sir."

Bodger was Halfhyde's servant, whom he had brought with him from the *Seahorse* by arrangement with the drafting authorities in the Portsmouth barrack hulks. "What happened?" he asked.

"You almost went over the side, sir. Mr 'Alliburton, 'e grabbed you in time like, sir. But you'd 'it your 'ead, sir, and passed out, and you was badly bruised elsewhere, sir."

"I see. And the ship, Bodger?"

"Safe, sir. Thanks to Mr 'Alliburton, sir. On course an' all shipshape . . . in a manner o' speaking, that is."

Halfhyde nodded, then winced as pain shot through his head. "I'd like words with Mr Halliburton, Bodger—"

"Yessir."

"But first a whisky, Bodger."

Bodger shook his head. "No whisky, sir. Mr 'Alliburton's orders, sir. You're on the sick list, like."

"I'm taking myself off it, Bodger. A whisky, and at once. I don't know what Mr Halliburton threatened you with if you disobey his order, but by God, Bodger, if you disobey mine, I'll have your fat carcass keel-hauled!"

"Yessir! Very good, sir! Whisky comin' up, sir!" Bodger stepped across to a cupboard; both it and its well-secured contents had survived the typhoon. Bodger poured a little whisky into a glass and handed it to Halfhyde, then went to summon the first lieutenant. When Halliburton came into his cabin, Halfhyde asked for his full report.

"All's well, sir. The turn was completed shortly after you hit your head, and I followed your earlier instructions—kept steerage way only, and held her there. It was a case of waiting, and the storm passed towards the north-west, just as you predicted." He added, "The weather's moderating now, sir."

"You've done well, Mr Halliburton. How long did it last?"

"Twenty-four hours, sir, till I came back on course."

"Damage?"

"Superficial, sir. Sea-boat torn adrift and smashed, some weather doors stove in, one of the torpedo-tubes twisted and out of action. I've sounded round all bilges and we're taking no water." The first lieutenant's voice became more sombre. "Four stokers and a leading stoker burned, sir, but not too seriously. Amongst the seamen, four broken arms and a broken leg, all splinted. One man washed overboard and not recovered— Leading-Seaman Hamilton. Nothing anyone could do in the sea that was running, sir."

Halfhyde nodded sombrely; no sea-boat could possibly have been sent away, and to have given such an order would have meant death for all its crew. Thus did seamen serve the Queen, and the loss was part of naval life, though none the less to be deplored. With a heavy heart Halfhyde said again, "You've done well, Mr Halliburton and I shall report as much to the commodore upon making my rendezvous."

"Thank you, sir," Halliburton looked pleased: words of praise had been rare enough. The captain seemed to have iron in his soul and vinegar in his veins, yet already it was obvious that he had the respect of the ship's company. He was someone to live up to.

Halfhyde gave his head a shake; the pain was leaving him and he needed fresh air to complete the cure. "I shall be on the bridge shortly, Mr Halliburton. If the land or any ship is sighted in the meantime, I am to be informed without delay."

"Aye, aye, sir." Halliburton turned away and left the cabin. Halfhyde listened to the heavy clump of feet as the first lieutenant ascended the ladder to the upper deck, then swung his legs from his bunk and stood up. For a moment there was a swimming sensation and he put out a hand to steady himself, but the moment passed and all was well. He called for Bodger to bring hot water for shaving. There was considerable motion upon the ship still and there was a shake in his hands, but a captain did not appear from his quarters unshaven. Shaved and dressed in oilskins, Halfhyde made his way along the upper deck, seeing the damage for himself. Another oilskinned figure touched a hand to the brim of his sou'wester, and Halfhyde stopped for a word.

"Good morning, Mr Stallybrass. I fear your tubes have suffered."

The torpedo-gunner, a warrant officer approaching fifty, nodded. "Aye, sir. We'll do our best, but it has the look of a dockyard job."

"There'll be no dockyard for us, Mr Stallybrass, unless the commodore orders us to Hong Kong, which is not likely in my opinion."

"No, sir. In any case, sir, torpedo-tubes'd not have been much use against them natives. All the way out from Pompey, sir, I've been wonderin' why they sent us."

Halfhyde smiled and laid a hand on the warrant officer's shoulder. "You must look beyond your torpedo-tubes, Mr Stallybrass. We're a handy vessel for inshore work with our shallow draught, and our guns, though small, can be threatening enough to a fleet of native canoes, with the cruisers lying off as the ultimate sanction." He continued along the deck for the navigating bridge, leaving Stallybrass to suck his teeth: with one tube useless, the torpedo-gunner felt fifty per cent emasculated, which was a tiresome feeling for a man nearing retirement who would dearly have loved to have fired off his tin fish in earnest on what would probably be his last commission afloat.

Throughout the rest of that day the weather continued to moderate as the typhoon departed on its north-westerly track towards Japan and China. There was a heavy swell left behind, but the surface itself was smooth and oily and the sun shone bright. All hammocks and mattresses, together with seasoaked clothing, were brought to the upper deck and rigged on lines to dry out. Halfhyde watched from the bridge.

"We have the look of a Chinese laundry, Mr Halliburton," he remarked.

"I'm sorry, sir."

Halfhyde smiled. "I was certainly not criticizing. I like a healthy ship's company, and a damp fug along the mess decks is to be deplored."

"Yes, sir."

Halfhyde turned to pace his navigating bridge, two steps one way, two the other: the space was small and cluttered. He looked fore and aft along his decks, where the seamen were still making good the storm damage. They were working well under their petty officers and leading hands: he had a good ship's company and was grateful for it. He said as much to Halliburton, and meant what he said. In the Royal Navy a lieutenant-in-command needed to run an efficient ship if he wished for promotion; and the extra pay attendant upon such eventual promotion would make life easier for an officer without private means . . . after a while he stopped to take a look at the chart. At noon, sights were taken by the navigating officer, Sub-Lieutenant Maxwell, and by Halfhyde himself. The sight placed *Talisman* within two hundred miles of her rendezvous; and as the sun began to go down that evening the masthead lookout reported a black smudge of land ahead, fine on the port bow.

Halfhyde glanced at the sub-lieutenant. "Well, Mr Maxwell?"

"Woleai Island, sir."

Halfhyde lifted his telescope and studied the distant land as, soon after, it came into view from the navigating bridge. He saw palms and sand, the latter red-gold as the sun moved lower. Then, a little to the west of the island, two more smudges came into the view of the masthead lookout, who sang out, "Two ships, sir, hull down on the port beam."

A few minutes later Halfhyde saw them. First the masts and funnels, then the great gun-turrets, yellow-painted like the rest of the upperworks, above light grey hulls: the colours of the China station. "The Long Range Squadron," he said. "Bring the ship round to join the commodore, if you please, Mr Maxwell."

Talisman altered to port and within the next ten minutes a signal lamp began winking from high up in the *Port Royal*. The yeoman of signals read it off.

"*Talisman* from Commodore, sir: *Welcome to my command. Report typhoon damage.*"

Halfhyde summarized the damage along his upper deck and indicated that he had non-urgent casualties. When the signal had been passed, another message came from the commodore ordering *Talisman* to take station in Line Ahead; and informing Halfhyde that a boat would be sent as soon after first light as a moderation in the dangerous swell might permit, to bring off the casualties for medical attention together with Halfhyde himself who was required to report for orders. As this signal was acknowledged, the torpedo-boat destroyer, closing the gap, steamed down the starboard sides of the great cruisers, Halfhyde standing at the salute in the fading light of near sunset as the boatswain's calls shrilled across and the bugles sounded in return. *Talisman* came round to starboard in rear of the line, taking up her position astern of the *Plantagenet*.

Next morning, a little after eight o'clock, by which time the swell had subsided sufficiently, Bassinghorn's squadron stopped engines and lay hove-to while Halfhyde and the casualties were pulled across in one of the *Port Royal*'s boats. Commodore Henry Bassinghorn was waiting in person at the head of the ladder as Halfhyde was piped aboard. When the salutes had been exchanged and the shrilling of the calls had died away, Bassinghorn held out his hand.

"My dear Halfhyde, I'm delighted to see you again."

"The pleasure's mine, sir."

"You've breakfasted, I take it?"

"Yes, sir, thank you."

"So have I. Come to my quarters—we'll not lose time." Bassinghorn turned away and Halfhyde followed. "I'm relieved the typhoon didn't incapacitate you, my dear fellow. My ships rode it well enough too, which is fortunate, for there's trouble ahead of us. I understand you're not in possession of all the facts, which is something I shall rectify." He said nothing further until they had reached his quarters aft, where he led the way past the Royal Marine Light Infantry sentry on guard by his outer door, through a small vestibule and into his day-cabin, a comfortable apartment furnished with highly-polished mahogany and chintz-covered easy chairs. Bassinghorn sat himself at his roll-top desk and gestured Halfhyde to one of the arm-chairs.

Halfhyde sat, and studied Bassinghorn covertly. The commodore had changed little over the years since they had last met; the hair of head and beard was a little greyer now, but that was all. There was the same vigour, the same sense of energy and purpose, the same integrity of character evident in the straight look of the blue eyes. Bassinghorn said, as though aware of Halfhyde's personal interest, "You may remember I once believed the time to be not far off when My Lords of the Admiralty would put me on the beach. I'm glad to say that was not yet to be."

"I'm glad too, sir. My belated congratulations on your promotion." Halfhyde spoke with genuine feeling. "The Admiralty came to their senses!"

Bassinghorn smiled. "I must live up to their expectations, Halfhyde. And you?"

"I have nothing to complain of, sir."

There was a pause, then Bassinghorn said, "Unusual—since I know you've served under the redoubtable Captain Watkiss!"

"More than once, sir."

There was a smile behind the commodore's beard and a twinkle in the eyes. "A most loyal officer."

"Most loyal, sir."

"But now, as I understand, put upon the half-pay list."

"I'm sorry to hear that, sir," Halfhyde said with sincerity: as one who had himself suffered the frustration of unemployment on the half-pay list, he would wish it upon no one else. In his case, real poverty had made it worse; Captain Watkiss wouldn't suffer that—he was a wealthy man, not dependent upon his pay. Halfhyde had kept a straight face at the mention of Watkiss's loyalty, which manifested itself mostly as a lunatic loathing of "dagoes" as he insisted upon calling all foreigners; but he had said no more. Bassinghorn would not expect him to, but had been human enough to show that he understood the difficulties and frustrations attendant upon service under Watkiss's command, difficulties and frustrations that might well have driven mad a lesser man than Halfhyde. The pleasantries over, Bassinghorn turned to his orders.

"Have you," he asked, "any experience of the South Sea islands? I believe you have not?"

"None, sir."

"But since leaving Portsmouth you'll have studied the Admiralty Sailing Directions for the area of Zanatu?"

"Yes indeed, sir."

Bassinghorn nodded. "As I would expect. You'll know that many of the islands are difficult of entry, that careful pilotage is necessary to avoid the reefs."

"Yes, sir. Also that Zanatu is worse than any."

"Exactly. Well, I have every confidence in your ability to handle your ship, Halfhyde. But the point is, it's going to be largely up to you—my cruisers cannot be hazarded in the lagoon except in an emergency. I am under very explicit orders on that score. The *Talisman* will be the link between myself and the island— and its Governor, Sir Wilbraham Carse, who is Her Majesty's representative in the group of islands. As you know, Zanatu is the largest and forms the seat of government."

Halfhyde nodded. It seemed his own prognostications as expressed to Stallybrass were being confirmed. To support this he asked, "Will my ship be used to put landing-parties ashore from your cruisers, sir?"

"Very likely, depending on how far matters develop. There is more than enough depth of water for a torpedo-boat destroyer to lie alongside the jetties, though not enough for a cruiser. However, in the first instance, I shall want you simply to land your own parties by use of your boats—I believe you reported that you'd lost only one boat in the typhoon?"

"Yes, sir."

"Good. Now, in brief, the background is this: a couple of renegade Australians landed on Zanatu some months ago—men believed to have been bandits, or bushrangers as the Australians call them. Their names are Dancey and Mulligan, both being of Irish extraction. These men have stirred up the native population to rebel against the Crown, and have brought with them a considerable quantity of arms and ammunition to lend weight to the natives' spears." Bassinghorn paused. "At the time I sailed from Hong Kong, the rebellion had in fact gone no further than a threat. But shortly before the typhoon hit, I was spoken to by a merchantman making for Shanghai from the south. Her master reported that he had been fired upon whilst attempting to enter the lagoon, and that he had read a semaphore message from the roof of the Residency. The building was under siege and lives had been lost. He was asked to abandon his attempt to enter and to make a report to the authorities as soon as possible, which he did."

"I see, sir." Halfhyde pulled at his long jaw. "What is the objective of these men, Dancey and Mulligan? Is this known?"

"Not known, only conjectured. I was told the Colonial Office believed they wish to make Zanatu into some kind of a stronghold for their own use, but for what special purpose remains a mystery—to me, at all events."

"A pirate lair, Captain Morgan all over again?"

Bassinghorn laughed. "Such would scarcely last for long today. Indeed, our own arrival is intended to put a stop to it once and for all."

"I believe we shall have little difficulty, sir."

"We would not have," Bassinghorn said quietly, "if it were not for another consideration, one that could put Zanatu, and my actions, in the centre of the world's stage."

Halfhyde lifted an eyebrow. "And that is?"

Bassinghorn said, "Intelligence has reached the Governor in Hong Kong that a Russian battle fleet has left Vladivostok for a southern destination." He met Halfhyde's eye and held it. "This fleet is commanded by Admiral Prince Gorsinski. It seems that history could be about to repeat itself so far as you and I are concerned. Prince Gorsinski is believed to be making towards Zanatu, where the Czar sees a possible foothold in the South Pacific . . ."

Halfhyde returned aboard the *Talisman* with plenty on his mind. If the interpretation placed in Hong Kong on Gorsinski's movements was correct, then Dancey and Mulligan were of little account in themselves. They were to be the cat's-paws for Russian expansion, and Gorsinski would be making use of a prepared position as it were, bringing his guns to threaten a British presence that was already under attack. The ways of kings and powerful statesmen were always devious. The Czar of all the Russias could pose as a liberator, a humanitarian who was going in via his kinsman Prince Gorsinski to succour a native people being oppressed by the British Empire's might, a people already in revolt against Queen Victoria. Far fetched perhaps, yet possible . . .

If so, then Commodore Henry Bassinghorn would need to walk a tightrope of decision and diplomacy, a tightrope that could give way beneath him at the whim of the Board of Admiralty or the Foreign Office, should he happen to make the wrong decision and use his guns before Whitehall was ready for the crash and thunder of war. Unless he was overtaken by a fast ship with orders, the whole conduct of operations would be up to him alone—if and when the Russian fleet arrived. Bassinghorn had believed they would; Czar Nicholas was anxious to extend

his sphere of influence in any way possible, and although Zanatu
would be unusable as a naval base for anything other than small
vessels, he could establish a military presence there, perhaps as
a stepping stone to further conquests in the area that would lead
to a Russian chain of small island bases across the whole of the
South Pacific to act, *inter alia,* as a threat against Australia and
New Zealand and to interfere with the Empire's trading links in
time of actual war.

As the engines of the Long Range Squadron turned over once
again on the commodore's order and the ships proceeded on
passage, Halfhyde acquainted his first lieutenant with the situation. He said, "The commodore intends to send us in ahead, to
probe the situation for ourselves and to try to establish contact
with the Governor. In the meantime, landing-parties are to be
detailed at once and the seamen and stokers exercised in cutlass drill by the gunner's mate. Exercised until they drop! All
boats are to be ready to proceed inshore at short notice. Gun
drill will be exercised during the passage, when ordered by signal from the commodore." He gave a hard laugh. "If we fall in
with Admiral Prince Gorsinski, you may well find yourself in
command before you expected it, Mr Halliburton—that is, if he
knows that I'm aboard the *Talisman!*"

Halliburton asked diffidently, "Why is that, sir?"

Again Halfhyde laughed, a sound of no humour. "Because
Gorsinski hates my guts, Mr Halliburton, that's why! I've encoun-
tered him too often in the past, have always bested him, and
caused havoc to his ships by various subterfuges and stratagems.
As a result, he is keen for revenge, Mr Halliburton. And like all
highly-placed Russians he is imperious . . . and few are so
highly-placed as he, since he is related by blood to the Czar
himself."

• • •

The squadron made its approach to Zanatu under cover of darkness, or such darkness as was available beneath the moon that shed its silvery light over the guns and bridges, masts and funnels and boats, over Mr Stallybrass's one undamaged torpedo-tube that might yet be used now. Stallybrass ran his fingers lovingly over the metal: with luck, he would have Prince Gorsinski's flagship in his sights before long . . . As he thought of war, war that he had been trained for during more than thirty years at sea, reaching back to the days of the old sailing Navy, he saw a blue-shaded light flashing back from the *Port Royal*'s bridge. No signalman himself, he was unable to read it off; but within a couple of minutes the order was being passed quietly round the ship.

"Landing-parties as detailed, fall in aft! The ship is under orders to enter."

Mr Stallybrass moved away from his torpedo-tubes and made his way aft to the quarterdeck. The landing-parties, of which he was to be second-in-command, began to muster with bayonetted rifles at the trail and cutlasses belted at their sides, gaiters fastened around the bell-bottoms of their white duck uniforms. As the vessel closed the entry to the lagoon, moving at slow speed now, the next order came down from the bridge: "Stand by all boats' crews, swing out your boats."

The *Talisman* moved on past the cruisers as the gripes were slipped and the boats eased out on the davits. In the chains to port and starboard the leadsmen stood ready to swing their leads and gauge the depth of water. From the bridge Halfhyde watched closely, using his telescope as the *Talisman* neared the outcrop of coral that formed the reef around the lagoon. Passing through the narrows in safety he let out a long breath of relief but knew that he couldn't relax his vigilance as the leadsmen passed back the soundings. It was Halfhyde's intention to stop engines and lie off the shore once he had reached the centre of the lagoon, when he would send away the landing-parties under the sub-lieutenant and Stallybrass; and he had just passed the order to Mr Dappers in the engine-room when there was a stutter of machine-gun fire from the shore and a rain of bullets swept his decks.

Chapter 3

"THE SEARCHLIGHT, QUICKLY!" Halfhyde had spoken to his officer of the watch. "Try to pick out where the firing came from." The shoreline was in shadow and the machine-gun had fallen silent. As the searchlight came on from the after part of the bridge and its beam swung inshore, Halfhyde called for'ard to his foredeck. "Number One gun, stand by!"

"Stand by, sir." It was the gunner's mate who responded.

"Have you any casualties for'ard, Petty Officer Luke?"

"No, sir."

"Thank God for that." Halfhyde looked along the shaft of light as it travelled the line of the shore ahead of his bows. He saw it steady on a number of spear-carrying natives grouped around a white man with a machine-gun. This man looked as if he were about to use the weapon again. Halfhyde took up his megaphone and shouted across the gap of water. "If you fire once more, I shall blow you to kingdom come with my main armament. I have you well covered."

An Irish-accented voice came back. "Bluff, mister. You won't fire on colonists."

"Try me. You've just fired on my ship. I'm well entitled to answer fire with fire, and shall do so."

There was a pause. The searchlight was held steady on the group of natives and their white leader. The shore was thickly wooded, with palm trees behind the moon-silvered sand; the group was half-concealed by palms that came down to the water's edge to the left of some shaky-looking jetties that reached out into the lagoon, no doubt for the off-loading of cargoes when supplies reached the island. The pause went on; no further talk was exchanged. Halfhyde began to sweat into his uniform. What he had said was true enough, but to open fire precipitately might rebound on Bassinghorn: the delicacy of his mission had to be borne in mind, and although the British Empire was well accustomed to the despatch of gunboats to resolve difficult situations, the hope was always that the threat would be enough. And, this time, he had so far suffered no casualties to his ship's company.

Halfhyde broke the silence. Using his megaphone again he called out, "I intend landing a party of seamen with orders to make contact with the Residency. They are not to be interfered with. My guns will remain manned." The decision taken, Halfhyde turned aft. "Mr Halliburton!"

"Yes, sir?"

"Lower the boats and embark the landing-parties, if you please. Send the sub-lieutenant up to me first."

"Aye, aye, sir."

Within half a minute the sub-lieutenant was on the bridge. Halfhyde said, "It's going to be a tricky business and you'll need your wits about you. You have my authority to use your rifles or cutlasses if you're attacked, but you're not to attack first. You know your orders: to make contact with the Governor and place yourself and the squadron at his disposal, then send a messenger to inform me of His Excellency's requirements. All understood?"

"Yes, sir, except for one thing—"

"Well?"

"If I'm denied entry to the Residency, sir, am I to—"

"Use force?" Halfhyde laughed. "You may consider that a

refusal of entry by the revolutionaries constitutes an attack upon you, Mr Maxwell, and act accordingly!"

There was a brooding silence after the boats had gone inshore. In the searchlight's beam, they had been watched from the *Talisman's* upper deck and bridge. Pulled quickly across the still waters of the lagoon, the men disembarked at the jetties and formed up on the sand. As the boats had left the ship, the white man, presumably either Dancey or Mulligan, had withdrawn into the trees followed by the natives. The beach was deserted. The Residency itself was visible in the moonlight, about half a mile behind the tree-fringed sand, standing on some rising ground. Maxwell should have no difficulty with his geography. Halfhyde ordered the searchlight to be switched off and paced his small bridge, back and forth; there was nothing he could do until either the fighting broke out ashore or Maxwell sent a message back. The inaction was hard to bear; Halliburton, realizing that his captain might snap if spoken to, maintained a nervous silence, standing before the binnacle so as to clear the after part for Halfhyde's pacing.

After some fifteen minutes rifle fire was heard, accompanied by shouts and cries, then a curious sound, almost like music from a deep-throated wind instrument, a rising and falling sound.

"What the devil's that?" Halfhyde said.

"I don't know, sir."

"It's a kind of ululation. Put the searchlight on the beach again, Mr Halliburton."

"Aye, aye, sir." The first lieutenant passed the order and the beam came on, fingering out across the water. It swept the beach, which was still deserted: it was an eerie scene, and somehow immensely foreboding in its very desolation. Halfhyde looked at the jetties through his telescope, examining them with more care than hitherto. They had a derelict look as of infrequent use; probably few ships ever entered the lagoon, perhaps only one in something like six months bringing in necessary supplies from the outside world. The islands would be largely self-supporting, and only the Governor's luxuries would need to be brought in. It would be a fairly idyllic existence except in times of revolt . . . dusky maidens, waving palms, long stretches of silver sand lapped by deep blue water . . . an ideal and undemanding appointment for a Governor said by Bassinghorn to be close to retirement: Halfhyde could not imagine that, until now, the Governorship of Zanatu and its islands had been an important post for a colonial servant of Her Majesty whatever value the Czar of all the Russias cared to place upon it in furtherance of his schemes. Possibly that was a family matter: Queen Victoria was not known as the milch cow of Europe for nothing. Czar Nicholas II was married to the granddaughter of Her Majesty, who could undoubtedly be a tiresome old lady when she chose and was ever inclined towards interference. Halfhyde grinned to himself: the loss of Zanatu would loom disproportionately large in Buckingham Palace as a smack in the face for grandmother-in-law.

"Off searchlight," he ordered. Once again, the beam died. The silence was more intense than ever. Then the weird noise— the ululation, if it was that—started again, rising and falling away, then mounting to a high pitch, becoming almost a frenzy.

Upon reaching the Residency compound, the naval party had found a strong force of natives, armed with spears and arrayed across the gate on the outside. When a number of spears had been projected towards the advancing men, Sub-Lieutenant

Maxwell at once ordered the rifles to open and half the seamen and stokers to go forward at the double under the covering fire and charge the line with cutlasses. He had scarcely given the order when a spear took him full in the chest. His body crashed to the ground and was at once scooped up by a giant-sized leading stoker and carried onward. As the charge went forward, more firing came from inside the compound, and the virtually naked natives, evidently not caring for the look of the brandished cutlasses, wavered. Behind them the gates were opened by some of the Residency staff, and the landing-parties cut their way through, hacking with the cold steel at necks and arms or slicing into stomachs to disembowel them bloodily. Four more men dropped to the lunges of the spears and were lifted and carried on to the order of Mr Stallybrass, now in command. There was a rising and falling sound from the natives, the curious howling that had been heard aboard the *Talisman*. The torpedo-gunner, sweating despite the comparative cool of the night air, felt a tingling sensation in his spine as he listened to the weird sounds behind him. Fervently he wished himself back aboard, back in the familiar surroundings of a British warship. In rear the gates were shut against the mob; the ululation continued, and now and again a spear was thrown. Mr Stallybrass ordered his men across the courtyard at the double and soon they had gained the cover of the Residency building, clumping up some steps into a spacious hall where a man, tall and elderly and white-suited, stood with a younger man upon whose shoulder he was leaning for support.

The torpedo-gunner went forward and saluted. "Are you His Excellency the Governor, sir?" he asked.

The old man nodded. "I am. I'm delighted to see you. The Navy can always be relied upon."

"Yes, sir." Stallybrass introduced himself. "Name o' Stallybrass, sir, torpedo-gunner. Are you all right, sir?"

There was a thin smile. "I shall survive, never fear."

"What force have you on the island, sir?"

Sir Wilbraham said, "Locally recruited police, loyal until recently. Now I have no force. They have turned against the Crown."

"All of them, sir?"

"Not all. Most of them. They have listened to foolish words. I owe my life to my personal staff and my servants."

"Native servants who have remained loyal, sir?"

The Governor nodded. "Yes. May I ask what your orders are?"

Mr Stallybrass brought out a large handkerchief and wiped it across his face. He said, "The orders to Sub-Lieutenant Maxwell, sir, now dead, were to make contact with you and place himself under your command, sir, and that's what I'm now doing in his place."

"Orders from whom?"

"From my captain, sir, Lieutenant Halfhyde, who derives his authority from Commodore Bassinghorn commanding the Long Range Squadron—"

"And Bassinghorn's ships—where are they?"

"Lying off outside the reef, sir. The heavy cruisers are too big to enter, sir, they draw too much water."

"Yes, quite."

"But they have their gun-batteries, sir. Six-inch breech-loaders, sir. A word from Lieutenant Halfhyde by signal will be enough, sir."

"No, no." His Excellency shook his head. "There must be no bombardment, Mr Stallybrass."

"It may be the only way, sir."

"Force is never the only way and I shall not permit a bombardment in which the innocent would suffer with the guilty."

"But if the Russians come—"

"That is a different consideration. Meanwhile the welfare of the islanders is my responsibility, and one that I shall discharge peacefully. They trust me, Mr Stallybrass, and I shall not bring them death and destruction."

"But I understood you asked for ships, sir—"

"Yes, indeed. But to bring order, not chaos. What is needed is a reinforced police action, Mr Stallybrass, not a military one. It's inevitable that even in a police action, of course, there will be casualties, but they must be minimal."

"Well, sir, if that's to be your order—"

"It is."

"Then it will be conveyed to my captain, sir." Stallybrass hesitated. "P'raps it would help, sir, if you told me the whole situation in detail before I send word back to my ship, that's if a message can be got through the natives outside the gates."

"If your ship has my roof in view, a message can be sent by semaphore," Sir Wilbraham said. "Come to my study, and I shall tell you a somewhat extraordinary story."

The study was a quiet place, book-lined and rather stuffy though the ceiling was high. Dawn was starting to come up now, and its light coming through from the verandah added to that of a paraffin lamp on the Governor's leather-topped desk. The torpedo-gunner was waved to a comfortable chair while Sir Wilbraham Carse stood with his hands behind his back, gazing from the window into the many colours of the sunrise. He told his story in a matter-of-fact voice; despite his having referred to it as an extraordinary one, it was obvious that to one like himself who had spent much of his latter life in the Pacific islands, it was not especially remarkable. Mr Stallybrass, however, more accustomed to the ways of Her Majesty's Navy and to the roistering life to be found in the naval ports of the Empire, found it incredible enough to ensure his close attention.

Sir Wilbraham, speaking slowly in his old man's voice, said that the two Irish-Australians, Dancey and Mulligan, had come to the islands some months before and at first had made no trouble for the British Crown; indeed, Sir Wilbraham had entertained them to sundowners and even to dinner on a couple of occasions until a ship had entered from Brisbane bringing two Australian policemen who had made enquiries as to their whereabouts. Dancey and Mulligan had disappeared from the moment the policemen had been seen to disembark, and thereafter no native seemed to know anything of their movements. The policemen had carried out a search aided by the local native police and had gone away empty handed. Then, six weeks before Bassinghorn's arrival, four police constables under an inspector had arrived, this time from Sydney; one after the other, over the next few weeks, they had been found murdered, each time with a spear pinning them to a tree and their bodies mutilated. It had proved impossible to get any statements from any of the inhabitants of Zanatu or the other islands; the native police were equally unhelpful. The Governor had been unable to get a report back to Australia, so no more police had been sent in. Then mysterious things began happening: a native had blown a hand off when trying to fire an ancient flint-lock pistol which he'd had no business to be in possession of; a number of natives had been seen to be wearing gold bangles and rings and necklaces of cheap, tawdry jewellery; gatherings had taken place at which animal sacrifices had been made before totem poles, gatherings at which no pains seemed to have been taken to keep the proceedings secret. Then there had been human sacrifices. This had indicated to the Governor that British authority was being deliberately disregarded, and a growing impertinence and insolence on the part of the native population had confirmed this. Sir Wilbraham and Lady Carse had themselves been subject to insult in public. The Residency had been attacked and lives had been lost. And still there was no overt sign of either Dancey or Mulligan.

"But they're behind it, you believe, sir?" Stallybrass asked.

The Governor nodded. "Oh, undoubtedly. That's why I shall not sanction a bombardment, you see. My people have been suborned; they are not themselves. Even though members of my staff have been killed, it would be totally wrong to make the natives suffer for what Dancey and Mulligan have done and are doing. Those two men must be cut out and got rid of and then we shall return to normal in the islands."

"Yes, sir. At what point, sir, did open rebellion start?"

Sir Wilbraham said, "About a month ago. The native police refused duty and the British officer in charge was killed—most brutally. From that time on, there has been no effective police force at all. Those that remained loyal came to me at the Residency, and as I have said, formed my only protection, my only guard together with my staff and servants. I cannot predict how long they will remain loyal, for the pressures are very great—indeed I would have said intolerable." He paused. "The families of these good men have suffered. Parts of bodies have been cast into the compound as proof. It has been horrifying. Quite horrifying."

"I can believe that, sir. What is it that the Irishmen want? Do you know, sir?"

"Power," the Governor answered. "Power and freedom from

arrest for crimes committed in the Australian colonies. Robbery, rape, murder have been among these crimes, I understand. Here in Zanatu they see a safe retreat—so long as they have the native population on their side, they are beyond the reach of the law. They can live very well, in ease and luxury and with women available as well."

"Until the gifts run out, sir?" Stallybrass suggested.

The Governor gave a sad, humourless laugh. "The fake gold, the rubbishy trinkets? I think you have not yet heard of the cargo-cults, Mr Stallybrass!"

Stallybrass frowned in some perplexity. "No, sir, I don't reckon as I have. What might they be, sir?"

The Governor turned from the window and moved across to his desk to extinguish the lamp. "We have light enough now," he said, "and we must not waste precious paraffin, for I cannot say when fresh supplies will reach Zanatu." Beyond the verandah the colours of the dawn were splendid, gold and purple, orange and green dappling the trees and making a prism of the sky and of the sea glimpsed beyond the tree fringe and the sand. Sir Wilbraham went on, "I'll try to explain briefly. It's crazy, of course, but it has to be reckoned with—it goes very deep indeed in the islanders' beliefs and traditions. What they believe is this: if they take pains to prepare for great riches and great power, it will come to them. If they believe implicitly and make ready, noth-ing can stop the arrival of what they call cargo, which in fact is much the same as we ourselves call cargo. Do you follow?"

"No, sir, not exactly—"

"Then I'll try again." The Governor lifted a hand and waved it towards the south-east of the island. "If you go down to that corner of Zanatu, or if you take a boat across to the other islands which in fact are not used by any shipping at all, you'll find jetties built out into the lagoons. Rickety jetties, useless jetties built of palm fronds and pieces of bark, largely—but yet *looking* like jetties. Jetties that one day, as sure as the sun rises, will take the cargoes that are to come and that will make the natives rich and happy and powerful. I repeat, it's a very deep belief, an inherited belief from a distant past. And Dancey and Mulligan have used it to their own ends."

"With the trinkets, sir?"

"Yes. There is a promise of much, much more when the cargoes come."

"Dancey and Mulligan will make them come, sir, is that it?"

"Partly. But more important is this: the cargoes will not come unless there is a man, an Englishman—or at any rate a white man—to draw them to the islands. For no well-authenticated reason, that man, that entirely mythical man, is known as John Frumm. When as a result of the islanders' belief and preparedness John Frumm comes, as he has been expected to do for perhaps hundreds of years, then and only then will the cargoes arrive at the prepared jetties. It's a simple philosophy and I dare say a great comfort to the islanders—they're a very child-like race, don't you know, basically good people and without vice. The idea of the cult has given no trouble in the past since no one has sought until now to use it for wicked purposes."

Stallybrass nodded. "So Dancey and Mulligan are claiming the mantle of this John Frumm, sir?"

"No, no. Not exactly. Neither of them is claiming actually to be John Frumm. There is another man . . . a man who is said to have arrived here before they came and whom the natives already believed to be John Frumm. Dancey and Mulligan are far too astute, it appears, to interfere with this belief by claiming that one of *them* is John Frumm. They have left this man with his high position, and claim only to be his friends and agents. Thus the power and prestige of John Frumm is largely conferred upon themselves as proxy."

"I see, sir." Stallybrass blew out his cheeks: it was all a very tall story to be believed by any torpedo-gunner in any ship of the Fleet, but Sir Wilbraham seemed convinced. "And this other man, sir? Do you know who he is?"

"No. No one knows anything about him at all. My information came from loyal policemen and from such of the families of my servants as were able to take refuge in the Residency just in time to save their lives. They know nothing of John Frumm's real identity or of how he got here, believing, with the rest of the islanders, that in fact he is the real John Frumm."

"And his whereabouts, sir?"

Sir Wilbraham shrugged. "Equally unknown to me. But one thing is certain, Mr Stallybrass: if this John Frumm can be found and revealed as an impostor, then I believe the rebellion would collapse and the Irishmen would be delivered into my hands."

Once again, Mr Stallybrass took out his handkerchief and wiped his face. His fingers shook a little; the study was a gloomy place and there was something like witchcraft in the air, and nasty practices alien to a seaman . . . murder and mutilation and human sacrifice were a very different kettle of fish from the clean sea and the thunder of the great gun-batteries in action. But his immediate duty was clear enough: his captain had to be informed fully, and it was all the very devil of a lot for a man to send by semaphore from the roof of the Residency.

Chapter 4

HALFHYDE PACED his bridge as he had paced it throughout the night. The dawn had shown nothing moving on the sand or in the thickly-growing trees behind. The roof of the Residency was bare; there had been no sound of fighting, no sound of anything in fact. The hours had dragged. Bassinghorn had approached no closer. No hastening signals had come from him, no harassment, for which Halfhyde was grateful even though he had known there would be none: Bassinghorn believed in allowing his juniors full discretion to handle a situation once the initial orders had been given. He trusted; which meant that he was never willingly let down.

Halfhyde's impatience grew. He paced on, then stopped suddenly and turned to his first lieutenant.

"Mr Halliburton, I am not built by God for damned inaction. I can lose nothing by taking my ship alongside, and when I have done so I shall be in a position to land more men as may seem necessary. Warn the ship's company, if you please."

"Aye, aye, sir."

"And if we strike uncharted coral, the leadsmen's livers will be cut out for my breakfast."

"I—I beg your pardon, sir?" Halliburton's face was a picture of startled incredulity.

"For God's sake, Mr Halliburton, I am not always to be taken literally, but if you continue to stare at me as though I were

Mephistopheles you should not consider your own damned liver too securely shackled to your intestines!"

There were shouts and cries from the distance as the *Talisman* came safely alongside the wooden jetty. As a precaution more seamen and stokers had already been mustered to back up the original landing-party and on hearing the sounds Halfhyde lost no time in ordering them ashore. Armed men poured down the brow, led by Halfhyde himself, the ship being left to the first lieutenant's charge. Halfhyde, his eyes gleaming at the prospect of action, was armed with a revolver and a cutlass, the latter swinging around his head as he went at the double up the sand towards the trees.

The sounds increased. There was someone crashing through the undergrowth, and more distantly the racket of sustained rifle fire. This was coming closer. Halfhyde went on like the wind, shouting encouragement at the men behind. As he reached the trees and plunged in, he saw four seamen, their white duck uniforms standing out sharply in the jungle green. He called out to them; as he did so, one of them crashed to the ground and Halfhyde saw the arrow sticking out from between the shoulder-blades. Glimpsing a native body, Halfhyde brought up his revolver and fired: the man went down screaming. Halfhyde ran on, keeping up his fire until the chambers were empty. Overtaking the white-clad seamen he hailed one of them. "What's the situation, and what are you doing out here?"

"Message from Mr Stallybrass, sir. We was under orders to get back aboard and report—"

"The message, quickly!"

"It's an unconscionable long 'un, sir—"

"Hold on to it, then," Halfhyde snapped with an oath. "I shall.

get it from Mr Stallybrass in person." He waved the men on. Ahead, he could now see a mob of natives spread out before the Residency gates, inside which the torpedo-gunner was to be seen with his landing-party, holding off the native mob and at the same time engaging their attentions in order to give his messengers their chance to get clear. Now, with more men coming in behind them, the natives began to waver and Halfhyde, seizing his opportunity, shouted his men forward at the charge. They doubled from the trees behind fixed bayonets, firing pointblank into the islanders' bodies and yelling like devils out of hell, burly men, many of them bearded, all of them filled with blood-lust. A few spears were thrown and a few arrows sped into the trees from the natives' bows, and then the seamen and stokers were on them and it was a case of hand-to-hand fighting, murderous and with no quarter given. Whenever there was the chance, the men inside the Residency compound added to the rifle fire. Mr Stallybrass stood by to open up the gate, and as Halfhyde's party fought through to it, he flung it open and the men crowded into the compound shoulder to shoulder. The gate banged to behind them and the securing bar was dropped into place. The men doubled across the compound and into the hall of the Residency, followed by the curious rising and falling sounds from the natives outside.

"Now, Mr Stallybrass, your report, if you please."

"Aye, aye, sir. I don't know as it's going to make any sort o' sense, sir, but—"

"I'll be the judge of that, Mr Stallybrass."

"Yes, sir." The torpedo-gunner's face was as red as any turkey-cock from his exertions and his white uniform was rumpled and filthy. He gave the story as told by the Governor; Halfhyde listened closely.

Before Stallybrass had finished Sir Wilbraham Carse appeared, and Halfhyde saluted smartly. He said, "Lieutenant Halfhyde of the *Talisman,* Your Excellency, arrived to your assistance. I have the details from my torpedo-gunner."

"They've no doubt strained your credulity, Mr Halfhyde!"

Halfhyde smiled. "Not too far, sir. I've read about the cargo-cults, and about John Frumm."

"Who is apparently upon this island."

"Yes. I understand you've no idea who he might be, sir?"

Sir Wilbraham shook his head. "None, I'm afraid."

"Then I shall be finding out, and soon. It will be my first priority. He should be apprehended before the Russian squadron arrives to complicate the issue." Halfhyde paused, looking down the steps and across the compound. The natives were still milling about the gate and waving their spears. "In the meantime I have casualties. It's too much to expect that you'll have a medical man available, sir?"

"Yes, indeed. My small staff does not run to such." Sir Wilbraham rubbed at his eyes: he was obviously tired and strained, looking not far from the end of his tether. "My wife . . . she's been doing what she can for Stallybrass's men, but she has no expert knowledge . . ."

"I'm grateful to her ladyship, sir. I shall send a message from your roof to my commodore, with your permission. He'll land a doctor and some sick-berth ratings, under guard of an armed party." Halfhyde paused. "You spoke of a small staff, sir—as for me, I've so far seen no British other than yourself. May I ask what your staff consists of?"

Sir Wilbraham spread his hands. "Apart from the domestics, all of whom are islanders, I have my ADC and my two secretaries and their clerks as my personal staff. That is to say, I *had.*

Both my secretaries died in the fighting earlier, when the natives entered the compound, and two clerks were lost as well."

"No other British subjects, sir?"

"No." Sir Wilbraham gave a wan smile. "We're a tiny enough outpost of the Empire, Halfhyde, and in all truth there has been insufficient work to fill the days of such staff as I had."

Halfhyde nodded. Even the official entertaining would no doubt have been on a small scale, just the occasional visiting dignitary . . . He gave a cough and went on, "The message to my commodore, sir. I believe the threat of his guns, if he should circle the island with his cruisers, might have an excellent effect in forcing the production of John Frumm, sir!"

The Governor shook his head. "A threat, perhaps. But I insist that the guns do not open, Mr Halfhyde."

"Why so?"

Sir Wilbraham repeated what he had said earlier to the torpedo-gunner. Halfhyde said, "We are now in something of a war, sir, and my commodore may consider himself as having assumed the overall responsibility. If so, then the use or not of his batteries will be his decision. Now if you will be so good as to show me how to reach your roof?"

Commodore Henry Bassinghorn paced his compass platform, deep in thought, as the sun lifted higher over Zanatu to bring with it the enervating heat of the day. He watched the cutter being pulled inshore from the *Port Royal* taking an assistant surgeon to the succour of the wounded men. The boat cut a white swathe through a sea of deepest blue. Not a breath of wind stirred and now there was no sound from the shore, which lay at apparent peace beyond its enclosing coral reef over which a low swell surged, lifting and falling like the weird sound that had reached out earlier to the ships of the squadron. Bassinghorn brought up his telescope and for a few moments studied the island with its palms and the thick jungle in rear; Halfhyde's lengthy semaphore message from the Residency lay upon his mind. The cargo-cults were an immensely powerful force in the South Seas and the white man laughed at them at his peril. His heavy guns were there to be used, they were the ultimate reason for the Long Range Squadron's existence; but, at least, unless the Russian turned up, they could be sledgehammers when rifles might be enough; and in any case it would be dangerous to fly in the very face of His Excellency the Governor's wish, to flout his authority. But there was a sense of frustration to which Bassinghorn found himself reacting strongly. He turned to the *Port Royal's* commander standing at his side.

"This John Frumm, Fortescue."

"Yes, sir?"

Bassinghorn shifted restlessly, pulling at his beard. "There have been many John Frumms throughout the history of the South Pacific. Some harmless enough, some mad, some dangerously ambitious for themselves. The latter's what we're faced with this time, as we know, but chiefly through the agency of the men Dancey and Mulligan. Of John Frumm, it seems, no one knows anything. Is he a renegade like the Irishmen, or is he simply being made use of? And who is he—and how in God's name did he get to Zanatu?"

Fortescue shrugged. "There could be many means, sir. A survivor from a shipwreck, a stowaway from a merchant ship entering from Australia or South America, such who would not be missed from the crew muster."

"Yes. He could scarcely have dropped from the sky, certainly! He could have been landed secretly from some pearling schooner, perhaps—there's no effective control on the movements of those people." Bassinghorn brooded, feeling a deep sense of unease as the cutter with its armed seamen vanished from view behind an arm of the land. He said abruptly, "Send for the gunnery lieutenant, if you please, Commander. We shall employ the time in gun drill."

In the Residency the sound of the bugles was heard across the water from the squadron. The Governor looked up sharply. "What was that, Mr Halfhyde?"

"For exercise, hands to general quarters, sir."

"For exercise?"

"Yes, sir. The commodore will be exercising his guns' crews of seamen and marines. As a prudent officer, he will wish to be ready . . . if matters should call for action."

"You've put my views to him, of course."

Halfhyde nodded, but said no more. Covertly from his chair in the study he watched the Governor. Sir Wilbraham was a prey to his nerves. There was a shake in his hands and a tic in his cheek. He was doing his best to stiffen himself with whisky; Halfhyde had stopped at one glass, but not Sir Wilbraham. Halfhyde caught the torpedo-gunner's eye and fractionally lowered one eyelid, jerking his head as he did so towards the decanter, which was standing with a jug of water on a table just inside the verandah. Mr Stallybrass understood; and a minute or two later he got to his feet and moved cumbersomely across the room towards the verandah. As he came abreast of the table, his cutlass swung out from his body. The decanter toppled over, and smashed on the verandah's stone floor. "Sorry, I'm sure, sir," Mr Stallybrass said, full of contrition and embarrassment.

"Damn you for a clumsy oaf! That was my last bottle."

"So you told me, sir," Halfhyde said. There was a strong smell of whisky. Halfhyde regretted the waste, for he was by no means averse to whisky when the occasion allowed. As the Governor glowered and shook, he went on crisply, "If you don't wish the squadron to open upon your island, sir, and bring the rebellion to a sudden end, then we must—"

"It is not to be done, d'you hear me?" Sir Wilbraham half rose from his chair, but fell back, his face as white as a sheet behind the sunburn, a sickly, yellowish look. "They are my islanders still, and—"

"I appreciate your reasons, sir, and respect them. But the rebellion must be ended. To end it peacefully if possible is my own wish and without doubt my commodore's also. Therefore John Frumm must be found and brought to book at once."

"Yes, I agree."

"I shall find him." Halfhyde got to his feet and loomed over Sir Wilbraham. "The people who told you of his existence must now be questioned. That is the only way."

"No. You must find another, Mr Halfhyde. I insist . . . I've told you already."

"That vengeance will be taken—I know! I much regret the fact that there will be families outside the Residency for use as hostages, but I must have the information and I propose to get it. You must rely upon me and my seamen to defend any hostages to the best of our ability, Sir Wilbraham." Halfhyde paused. "I must ask you to send for your informers, if you please."

"I shall not."

Halfhyde took a deep breath. "Sir, you have a duty to Her Majesty, who will not wish to lose the islands. If Admiral Prince Gorsinski should arrive with his battleships, he will not respect your wish to preserve the natives. In the name of the Queen, sir, the present situation must be resolved before the Russians come. We must meet Gorsinski as a united force of British ships and loyal colonists, which we shall not do if John Frumm is not found. Kindly see sense, sir!"

It took a little more time but at last, recognizing the determination in Halfhyde, Sir Wilbraham conceded. The native informers were sent for: one policeman and three females from the domestic quarters, one of whom was the policeman's sister. The other women had parents outside the Residency. The policeman, who had been on duty inside the compound when the gates had first been stormed by the mob, had two more sisters somewhere on the island but, according to Sir Wilbraham, he was intensely loyal to the British Crown. Halfhyde called for the assistance of the ADC, the young man who had been in attendance on the Governor on the arrival of Stallybrass and the first landing-party—one Captain MacDonald, on secondment from the Royal Highland Regiment, the Black Watch.

MacDonald conducted the questioning, but after a while it became obvious that he was achieving nothing. The Polynesian native could be as obstinate as Sir Wilbraham Carse, it seemed.

"The threat to the families is inhibiting them?" Halfhyde asked.

"Yes, that's it. They don't believe you can protect them." The Scot grinned. "Frankly, neither do I! Which means I can understand their disbelief and their reluctance."

"Possibly," Halfhyde said grimly. "Keep on trying."

MacDonald did, still with no result. There was much chatter and many gesticulations, many rolling eyeballs, but nothing beyond what was already known, the bare facts that John Frumm had arrived and was about to bring down the blessings of God upon the islands and their inhabitants. There would be no more need for work.

"They do precious little anyway, I imagine," Halfhyde said with a laugh.

"Quite. But none at all is better than doing any."

"In other words, they're believers in John Frumm? It's not just their families' welfare?"

MacDonald nodded. "The belief's deep and implicit, bred into them. The Promised Land has come. They won't tell us anything, Halfhyde, I'm certain of it."

"Yet they spoke to His Excellency in the first place."

"Only to say that John Frumm had arrived. I believe it was a form of—of boasting if that's the word—"

"Saying yah boo to the British?"

"Something like that."

Halfhyde said, "They need some persuasion, it seems. Mr Stallybrass?"

"Yes, sir?"

"Your cutlass, Mr Stallybrass."

"My cutlass, sir?"

Halfhyde fractionally lowered an eyelid. "You're a man of iron, are you not, Mr Stallybrass, a man of blood and guts?"

"Yes indeed, sir."

"Quite! So you'll lay your cutlass where it'll do the most good, if you please—across the throat of one of the women. Captain MacDonald, a word in your ear." Halfhyde drew the soldier across the room and spoke in a low voice. "I'm not as bloodthirsty as my words. A touch of cold steel works wonders as a threat, and Mr Stallybrass is as full of harmless bluff as any good warrant officer in the Service."

At that moment, as if in proof of Halfhyde's words, the torpedo-gunner lifted his cutlass and cut through the air with it. There was a new tautness about the natives now, a wary, frightened look in their eyes as the torpedo-gunner advanced behind a magnificent stomach. Approaching one of the women and using just one hand, Stallybrass forced the mouth open and laid hold of the tongue, drawing it past the teeth. With the other hand he brought up his cutlass and put the edge across the writhing tongue. He put his face close; the woman's eyes rolled in terror.

"No talk now," Stallybrass said, "means no tongue to talk later. See, do you?"

"Mr Stallybrass." Halfhyde moved across. "She'll not talk with her tongue out—give her a chance. Let it snap back in for a moment."

"Aye, aye, sir." The torpedo-gunner let go, and the woman began screaming. Mr Stallybrass stopped her by laying the cutlass blade across her mouth. "Talk," he said. "John Frumm. Where is John Frumm? *Where—is—John—Frumm?*" He shifted the blade to the throat, laying it across the windpipe. The other woman was staring in abject terror, her breath coming in gasps and a hand to her lips. She would be next if the first woman didn't utter. Halfhyde was about to put some pressure of his own on her when a seaman from the torpedo-gunner's landing-party entered.

"Captain, sir."

"Yes?"

"A signal by light from the commodore, sir. Smoke has been sighted, sir, approaching from the north."

Halfhyde swore. "The devil it has! Are there any orders from the commodore?"

"No, sir. Just the information, sir."

Halfhyde nodded. "Thank you." He turned to the torpedo-gunner. "I'm going to the roof, Mr Stallybrass. The matter has now become vital and immediate. You will do what is necessary to extract the information."

His Excellency owned a telescope; on his way to the roof, Halfhyde borrowed it. Sir Wilbraham accompanied him, looking more strained than ever. Bassinghorn's squadron could be seen, lying off and lifting a little to the ocean swell, the ships' engines moving now and again to keep them in position: there was far too great a depth of water beneath them to allow of anchoring. Plumes of smoke were to be seen over the horizon's rim, and then funnels, and then the fighting-tops of what were clearly Russian warships.

Halfhyde glanced at the set face of the Governor. "A tricky situation is approaching, sir," he said.

"Disastrous!"

"Come, sir, that is an extreme word to use. Difficulties exist only to be overcome! Prince Gorsinski will first try the diplomatic approach. He will have to be outwitted, that's all."

"And when he has been outwitted, what then? Does he simply steam away? Or does he turn the tables by opening upon Bassinghorn's ships?"

The question was rhetorical; Halfhyde gave no answer beyond a shrug of his shoulders. Rationally, Prince Gorsinski could be supposed not to wish to provoke a war with Great Britain; but Gorsinski was not a rational officer. He had all the arrogance, all the impetuosity of his birth as a Russian aristocrat. He was not the sort ever to turn away with his tail between his legs. He was a man of cruelty and foul temper, detested by the officers and men under his command; and he had too often in the past been given his come-uppance by the British Navy—and by Halfhyde in person. As the Russian ships came nearer Halfhyde felt a wateriness in his stomach: there was immense danger to himself in the approach of Prince Gorsinski. His mind went back to the Bight of Benin in West Africa where he had encouraged a mutiny aboard Gorsinski's flagship *Romanov,* which had subsequently been blown up by her own company. Then a simple stratagem of Halfhyde's had brought about a collision and the grounding of the *St Petersburg* and the *Grand Duke Alexis.* He remembered the strange volcanic island that had sprung from the Pacific south of Parece Vela Island, where Gorsinski's armoured cruiser *Ostrolenka* had, by a freak of nature rather than any act of Halfhyde's, been imprisoned for ever in an inland lake following an upheaval of the sea bottom; and the Crimea and the Black Sea where Halfhyde, despite the antics of his commanding officer, Captain Watkiss, had cut out the British merchantman *Falls of Dochart* from under Gorsinski's nose and had encompassed the grounding of the *Nikolayev* off the entry to the Bosporus. Gorsinski was not a forgiving man . . .

Studying the Russian approach through the Governor's telescope, Halfhyde saw the flaunting Imperial ensigns, with the admiral's flag of Prince Gorsinski flying from the foretopmast head of a battleship which he identified as the *Catherine the Great.* With the flagship were two armoured cruisers, *Smolensk* and *Berezina.* When the Russian squadron was some six miles off the island, a signal lamp winked from the *Catherine the Great's* flag deck; watching, Halfhyde saw the acknowledgement from the *Port Royal.*

He lowered the telescope and closed it with a snap. "The time is short," he said crisply. "I had hoped Prince Gorsinski would allow us a longer breathing-space, but it seems that was not to be. It is now of the utmost urgency that John Frumm should be found and brought in."

Leaving Sir Wilbraham's presence, he strode away, making his way down to where the interrogation of the natives was taking place. To his immense relief, the torpedo-gunner was able to report success.

"They got the wind up, sir. Cutlasses is nasty things, sir, or can be."

"Well, Mr Stallybrass?"

"That there John Frumm, sir. He's down by the south-east corner, in a cave—"

"Guarded?"

Stallybrass nodded. "Guarded, yes, sir, but respectfully. More like a guard of honour as I understand. The native policeman will guide us there, sir, after dark."

Halfhyde clapped the torpedo-gunner on the shoulder and smiled. "Good work indeed, Mr Stallybrass—and I can only hope that after dark will prove soon enough!" He paused then added, "Is there any information about the Irishmen, Dancey and Mulligan?"

"No, sir. I believe the natives genuinely don't know."

"They may be found with John Frumm," Halfhyde said musingly. "We must be on the watch for that." Ordering the release of the islanders, he walked out into the compound. The mob was still massed outside the gates: that mob had a look of permanence. To get clear of the Residency was going to be difficult but would be achieved; the British Navy was well used to solving difficulties. The ululation started when Halfhyde was observed, a chilling sound coming from the shadow of the trees. Halfhyde went back inside the building, intending to snatch some sleep—he had had none during the night, and would have none during the forthcoming hours of darkness. At his request the ADC provided sleeping billets for the off-watch seamen and stokers, and rooms for himself and Stallybrass to use as required. Halfhyde had slept for two hours when he was brought awake by an urgent voice.

"Captain, sir!"

Halfhyde opened his eyes and sat up in bed. A seaman messenger had come. "What is it, Tubbs?"

Able Seaman Tubbs said, "Signal from the commodore, sir. He's sending a boat to take you off to the *Port Royal,* sir."

Halfhyde tumbled out of bed and within half an hour warlike sounds were heard as a strong guard of armed bluejackets from the *Port Royal* began to approach from the direction of the jetty. There was firing but it appeared to be aimed over the heads of the islanders, and there was no return of hostilities from the massed natives. They appeared somewhat cowed, Halfhyde thought, as though the appearance of yet more big ships and heavy guns was giving them pause. In the centre of the escort he left the Residency compound for Bassinghorn's boat at the jetty. He prayed that he might remain anonymous during the trip out to the *Port Royal;* no doubt Bassinghorn would have sent a picket-boat so that he could remain closeted in its cabin. He was not over worried; although Prince Gorsinski would almost certainly have a copy of the British Navy List aboard his flagship, Halfhyde's last-minute appointment to the command of *Talisman* was unlikely to have been included, but that anonymity must be preserved or his life wouldn't be worth a candle.

The march was made without incident; and on arrival at the jetty Halfhyde was relieved to see that all was well aboard the *Talisman,* with Halliburton in evidence on the quarterdeck. Halfhyde gave him a wave and called out, "Mr Halliburton, if you should be contacted by Prince Gorsinski, I am not your captain. You have no knowledge of any Halfhyde. Your captain's name is anything you fancy, but let us decide upon Smith. You understand?"

"Yes, sir," Halliburton answered doubtfully.

"Good!" Halfhyde stepped into Bassinghorn's boat—it was indeed the steam picket-boat—and was taken out across the lagoon, out through the entry channel and over the blue Pacific towards the *Port Royal's* starboard after ladder. He remained firmly in the cabin, head down. The Russian ships were keeping a safe and seamanlike distance from the British cruisers, but one glimpse of Halfhyde in Gorsinski's telescope and the grab would be swift and never mind Queen Victoria. For Halfhyde had swung from Gorsinski's upper yard-arm once before, and had only been saved from hanging by a miracle. God might not love his humble servant enough to send down another.

Chapter 5

HALFHYDE went aboard to the shrilling of the boatswain's calls and was taken below to the commodore's quarters in the stern.

In the day-cabin, Bassinghorn was standing looking out through a square port towards the Russian ships. He turned at Halfhyde's knock, and nodded a welcome. He looked worried, as well he might.

"Well, my dear fellow, we have matters to discuss. But first your report of events ashore."

Bidden to sit, Halfhyde gave his account of the situation around the Residency. He said, "I have information as to the whereabouts of the man said to be John Frumm, sir. I intend, with your permission, to seek him out tonight."

Bassinghorn pulled at his beard. "You have my permission and I wish you success, Halfhyde. But I'm far from convinced that he'll bring the solution to the Russian problem!"

"Possibly not, sir, but I believe it's important to try to bring the islanders back to their British loyalty before we confront Prince Gorsinski. John Frumm represents the best way of doing that, in my view."

Bassinghorn was in full agreement with that. "Now, the reason I sent for you. There has been an exchange of signals between Gorsinski and myself."

"Yes, sir?"

"Amicable enough to be sure. That is, so far." Bassinghorn gave a humourless smile. "Gorsinski offers his condolences and his Czar's upon our troubles with the islanders. He asks if he can be of assistance."

"The devil he does!" Halfhyde said tartly. "And may I ask what your reply was, sir?"

"It was polite, Halfhyde. I thanked him, but said that we were well able to cope with our own affairs—on behalf of Her Majesty. I thought I would add as a reminder, that we are here on Admiralty orders."

"Yes, indeed, sir." Halfhyde frowned. "Assistance . . . I imagine Gorsinski takes us for fools, as he has done in the past. One would think he had learned differently by now. Once he had put landing-parties ashore—"

"Quite. He must have known I would refuse. It was simply the opening ploy in the diplomatic game—and I fear I'm not a diplomat, my dear fellow!" Bassinghorn chuckled. "When his next signal came, my reply was a little more pointed."

"And his signal, sir?"

"It verged upon impertinence. The British, he suggested, appeared to have outstayed their welcome in the islands. Change, he said, was in the air. I replied bluntly that my guns would maintain the status quo."

"You have fewer than Prince Gorsinski, sir."

"True," Bassinghorn said sharply, "but that has never been an excuse for the Navy to refuse battle."

"As to that, sir, I agree, of course, and I was not suggesting that we should do so if matters go that far. But I do suggest that we use up the peaceful methods first."

Bassinghorn got to his feet again and walked across to his square port. He stood for some moments in frowning study of the great ornately-decorated ships with their Russian ensigns floating above the guns. He would be in no doubt that if the guns were used, his squadron would stand virtually no chance. Three ships to three, certainly, if Halfhyde's *Talisman* was included, but the total gun power of the Russian squadron was vastly superior to his own—and one of the Russians was a line-of-battle ship, strongly armoured in addition to being very heavily gunned. Bassinghorn came away from the port and stared down at his visitor.

He said, "I've had full discussions with my captains before sending for you, Halfhyde. My ships are ready when needs be and I shall never permit Gorsinski a foothold upon Zanatu or the other islands. That is my final word upon the matter."

"Of course, sir."

"Nevertheless, I need your counsel for two main reasons. Firstly, because you're *au fait* with the situation ashore and have had contact with Sir Wilbraham. Secondly, because you have a close personal knowledge of Prince Gorsinski."

"I have indeed, sir, to my regret. The man is a devil in more-or-less human form."

"My first point first. His Excellency—what are his intentions, Halfhyde?"

Halfhyde shrugged. "To safeguard his islanders—largely from any threat from your guns, sir, as I reported earlier."

"But as to the Russians?"

Halfhyde said, "He didn't pronounce on that point, sir. I raised it, but formed the impression that he hoped they wouldn't come, and that if they did, they would go away again!"

Bassinghorn glowered, bearded chin thrust forward. "A somewhat pusillanimous response."

"His Excellency has grown pusillanimous with age, I fancy. He has been under much strain, and now there is a shortage of whisky."

"He's taken to the bottle?"

"Only recently I believe, sir. I have seen to it that it will not continue."

Bassinghorn gave Halfhyde a sharp look. "From what you say, my conclusions are that we shall get little support from His Excellency. Am I right?"

"I think so, sir. He's cracking up, and he doesn't want to see years of conscientious work go for nothing in the holocaust of the guns." Halfhyde added, "I confess I have some sympathy for him."

"Yes, so perhaps have I, but the security of the Empire and of our trade routes must come first. That is the duty I am charged with." Bassinghorn stiffened, standing straight and tall, hands clasped behind his back. "Now—Gorsinski. Do you believe that in the last resort—or sooner—he'll risk involving his Czar in war?"

"Yes, sir, without a doubt, if he sees the islands as important to Russian interests, which clearly he does. Russia is set to expand, as we know, and has a formidable offensive potential. Besides, we must take Prince Gorsinski's own character into account. The very fact of your squadron standing between himself and his vanity as it were—that alone would be enough to project him into action, wholesale war or not. And he has quite enough connections at the Russian court to ensure that he's not unduly censured afterwards." Halfhyde paused, then asked, "Is there to be personal contact between you and Prince Gorsinski, sir?"

Bassinghorn said, "He has asked me to go aboard his flagship. I have refused, and have not invited him to come to my ship. The islands are ours, and are not to be a subject for barter—for discussion or compromise. I believe that to meet Gorsinski would be seen as weakness and doubt on my part."

• • •

Halfhyde was taken back to the lagoon. Bassinghorn's attitude
in refusing to see Gorsinski could be considered stiff-necked,
but Halfhyde believed the commodore to be correct. The British
ships were there by right, the Russians were not. The Russians
were interlopers and in basis there was, as Bassinghorn had said,
nothing to discuss. Nevertheless, when dealing with Gorsinski
it was as well to be wily rather than peremptory, and at least a
meeting might have acted as a procrastinator. Too late now:
Bassinghorn was not the man to go back upon a decision.

Once again under strong escort, Halfhyde marched back to
the Residency. The situation seemed as before; the natives let the
naval party through the gate without hindrance, though the
keening started on their approach and the eyes above the shaken
spears were angry and threatening. Inside, Halfhyde sought out
the Governor to report on his visit to the commodore. There
had been, Sir Wilbraham said, no overtures from the Russians,
no contact at all. He said, "If Prince Gorsinski should send a
boat into the lagoon, I would be prepared to meet either him
or his representatives. It would be only civil, I think."

"But possibly dangerous, sir. In any case, my commodore
would not allow the Russians to land."

Sir Wilbraham raised his eyebrows. "He would intercept, do
you suppose?"

"Yes, sir."

"But if I was prepared to meet them . . . if, say, I had invited
Prince Gorsinski as my guest?"

Halfhyde said cautiously, "That might, perhaps, put a different complexion on the matter. No doubt in normal times it would
be usual enough for you to entertain a member of the Russian
Royal family—a mere matter of diplomatic politeness—"

"Yes, most certainly."

"But the times are not normal, sir, far from it. You could not guarantee the safety of your important guest. I think the adherents of John Frumm would make little distinction between nationalities at this moment!"

Sir Wilbraham nodded. "Yes, there is that, of course."

"I would suggest, sir, with respect, that you issue no invitation, at least not without consulting Commodore Bassinghorn. If I may offer my opinion, it is currently a time for displaying what one might call a masterly inactivity. We must first see which way the wind blows, and it is up to Prince Gorsinski to blow before we do!"

"Perhaps, perhaps." Sir Wilbraham seemed relieved to be offered a deferment of decision-making, to have Halfhyde to lean upon. "In the meantime—"

"In the meantime, sir, John Frumm," Halfhyde said briskly. "But not until the dark comes down—and not in uniform. I shall adopt a disguise, with the help of your native staff." He coughed. "Before then there is another duty, a sad one."

"Yes?"

"The dead must be buried. The sun is strong."

Halfhyde walked away from the burials with head bent, thinking morbid thoughts. It was far from the first committal service he had read, but all the others had been at sea where the bodies of seamen who had died on active service had slid into the cool, clean waters that had been their life. The earth was different, more claustrophobic. Halfhyde thought of worms and decay. There was no padre attached to the Residency; the Church of England had few devotees in the islands around Zanatu, none indeed but the Governor with his family and personal staff. But many years earlier a roving bishop had consecrated some ground and Sub-Lieutenant Maxwell and the dead seamen, three of them, were laid to rest in a plot behind the Residency alongside two previous Governors and a number of young children who in years past had succumbed to the heat and the lack of medical attention. Halfhyde gave an involuntary shiver: to die in Zanatu would be horrid indeed, yet the possibility had to be faced.

The day wore on; the sun began its decline and the heat lessened as the shadows spread over the island. So far there had been no further overtures from the Russian squadron, the only movement taking place during the afternoon when boats had been sent away from all three ships to pull round in circles, uselessly. Halfhyde reflected that exercise was one thing, but to put boats' crews through the hell of heavy work during the afternoon's blistering heat was quite another and was probably due to Prince Gorsinski's venting his ill-temper on his men. Admirals and captains in the British Fleet were usually more humane, and more responsive to the sufferings of the lower deck, where comfort was never present. Gorsinski, who had once survived a mutiny, seemed to have learned little as a result. When British seamen had mutinied at Spithead it had been against an insensitive Board of Admiralty rather than against their own seagoing officers. Since then, largely, Nelson's prayer before Trafalgar had been taken to heart: "Let mercy, after victory, be the predominant feature in the British Fleet." Not so with the disdainful Russian aristocracy . . .

At last the full dark; moonlit, but as dark as it would get. With the assistance of Captain MacDonald and the native policeman who was to guide him to John Frumm, Halfhyde made ready. His body was darkened with boot blacking and he was dressed in a loin-cloth taken from one of the native servants and equipped with a spear and a bow-and-arrows which he would carry slung from his shoulder. His hair was cropped close to his scalp with scissors wielded by Lady Carse.

MacDonald said, "At a distance, you'll do. Close, you'll stand out a mile."

"I'm aware of that. It's a subterfuge to get me safely into the vicinity, nothing more than that."

"And when you get there?"

"I shall lie low, and I shall watch."

"And then?"

Halfhyde shrugged. "That must depend upon the situation as I find it. Beyond that, I have no plans laid."

"I wish you'd take some of your men," MacDonald said.

Halfhyde made a deprecatory gesture, and laughed. "A squad of good British jack-tars tramping their unhandy way through the jungle is not my idea of secrecy and a clandestine approach! The moment word of their coming was reported ahead of them, I would expect some rapid withdrawal on the part of John Frumm, involuntary or otherwise. No, my dear fellow, I am much better equipped if alone apart from the guide."

As soon as he was ready, the policeman, who had exchanged his British uniform jacket and shorts for native attire, if attire it could be called, led the way from the rear of the Residency, keeping close to the stockade and skirting the burial plot with its fresh graves, and through the trees towards a stout gate secured with a heavy iron bar set into brackets on either side. Outside, as Halfhyde had been told, a rebel native sat on watch with a spear. This man could summon help quickly from the islanders still clustered outside the main gate in the front. It was vital that his despatch should be as instantaneous as possible.

Halfhyde and the policeman made their approach with immense care, hidden from the moon by the trees and by the thick stockade itself. They made no sound that would be heard above the water-movement as the restless Pacific surged over the coral; just a few faint cracklings of sun-dried undergrowth beneath Halfhyde's bare feet.

Close to the stockade several tall trees grew.

Halfhyde looked up: the moon was bright, silvering the stockade and trees, but that was a chance that had to be taken. Praying for heaven's connivance in a good cause, he swarmed up the trunk until his head was just below the level of the top of the staves. It was a somewhat painful business, with no clothing between his skin and the roughness and protuberances of the bark. Easing his neck upwards, he peered cautiously over to the ground below. The native was squatting there, his spear across his knees. He had noticed nothing. Halfhyde withdrew his head and very carefully, very slowly, moved a little higher up the tall trunk. The policeman was below him now, climbing equally silently. Halfhyde sent up another prayer: that the policeman wouldn't suffer a shift in his loyalties once he was on the other side of the stockade. He believed he would not; the Residency still held one of his sisters. The cargo-cult faction was not the only one with hostages.

Just for a second Halfhyde remained poised over the top of the stockade. Then he dropped. It was all soon over. In the last split-second the islander beneath him became aware of danger and looked upwards. The face reacted in sudden terror but the man had no chance to utter a sound. Halfhyde landed fair and square on his shoulders and the neck snapped clean; he made no sound even in the act of dying. Halfhyde stood up, dusted his hands together, and beckoned to the policeman, who dropped and landed neatly beside him. The body was hidden quickly in the undergrowth and then, as carefully and quietly as before, they made their way around the stockade, keeping well clear of the cluster of natives at the main gate, and headed towards the south-east of the island in the close shelter of thick jungle.

They had seven miles to go; by Halfhyde's reckoning, it could take them as much as three to four hours, perhaps longer, to thrust through such difficult country. He would have preferred an approach by water, but a boat would have stood out a mile. Swimming? Halfhyde was an exceptionally strong swimmer and the distance would in any case be less, for, according to the policeman, the land route skirted a deep bay which could be quickly crossed by water. But the strong probability of sharks had precluded this. There was a shark net rigged across the entry through the reef, lowerable when vessels wished to enter; this was already lowered when Halfhyde had brought the *Talisman* in and, with discipline slipping on the island, had been lowered for some time before; by now the lagoon could be filled with sharks.

Halfhyde went doggedly forward behind his guide, his bare flesh tormented by flailing fronds that whipped back against him; insects crept and crawled horribly, unnamed beastliness slithered across legs and feet. Nature croaked and honked and twittered around and above him. There was a horrible damp-ness from past rains, and now and again he sank into boggy morasses and felt the revolting attentions of leeches as he drew himself out covered with foul, clinging mud. There was a stench of rot, of evil, of strange rites and weird practices, of heathen gods and idols, of sacrifice and terrible death. The moon, no doubt shining still, failed utterly to penetrate the dismal jungle and Halfhyde found it immensely difficult to keep his guide in view. The native policeman was moving with total sureness, knowing every inch of the route, and had no doubt chosen the easiest path through the jungle.

What the other parts must be like was beyond Halfhyde's imagination.

He tried to project his mind to happier surroundings, more congenial atmospheres: the compass platform of a ship in a seaway, the bridge personnel fighting clean elements; the fo'c'sle of a cruiser as she cut through blue water to leave a swirling white wake behind, stretching homeward when outward bound on foreign service; the majesty of a battle squadron entering Plymouth Sound or the Grand Harbour at Malta, the bugles blowing and the divisions fallen in fore and aft as the fifes and drums of the marines beat out *Rule, Britannia;* the splendidly autocratic sight of a post captain of the Royal Navy in gold-ringed frock-coat and starched shirt-cuffs standing with telescope beneath his arm as he waited at a spotless gangway to welcome an admiral aboard to the wail of the boatswain's calls.

Halfhyde came back to the uncomfortable present; this wouldn't last for ever. The splendour of the Fleet was still there and he would bask in it once again—if he lived!

He pressed on, swearing beneath his breath.

The policeman stopped and put a hand on Halfhyde's arm as he came up; for some distance now the going had been a shade easier, and there was some light ahead—the moon, shining down brightly on the sand fringing the lagoon.

"Well?" Halfhyde asked.

The native said something unintelligible and pointed ahead. Then he moved on again. Halfhyde followed, wondering what the man had pointed out. Soon after this, they reached the jungle's end. They looked out on the slope of the sand and the guide uttered again and pointed across the sand towards what looked like a cliff—rock at any rate, Halfhyde saw. He picked out a darker patch in the rock: it could be a cave.

"Well?" he said again.

The policeman said, "John Frumm."

"In the cave—there?" Halfhyde pointed. The man didn't appear to understand the words, but nodded vigorously at the gesture. Then he turned aside, beckoning Halfhyde to follow again. Back into the shelter of the jungle, though remaining now on the fringe, they headed round the sand. The obvious intent was to come up to the northern side of the cave: an area of the jungle, as Halfhyde had seen, extended almost to its entrance and he would be able to make his approach, with any luck at all, unseen until the last moment. Earlier questioning of the policeman by MacDonald had brought forth the assurance that during the night hours the guard on John Frumm was maintained by the women; it was, as Mr Stallybrass had already stated, more of a guard of honour than anything custodial. John Frumm was much trusted, much respected, and the night was the women's time: John Frumm was very much a male god and as such, and in order to keep his goodwill, he must be allowed the free run of any desires he might have. Halfhyde had no doubts that he could deal with the women so long as he could persuade them to keep quiet and not bring in their menfolk by unseemly screams when he appeared.

"Right," he said when they had reached the final jungle limits. "Now I go in alone . . . savvy?" The native nodded but looked as uncomprehending as before. Halfhyde blew out a long breath and added, for what it might be worth, "Stay here until I call you. *Here.*" He pointed down at the earth, firmly. "Until I

call." He pointed to his mouth. The policeman grinned and nodded again. Hoping for the best, Halfhyde turned away and
approached the rock, which was immensely high. Keeping close
against it, he sidled along towards the mouth of the cave. At the
entry he stopped and listened. There was no sound: the silence
could almost be felt.

Then there was a sudden snore, a long-drawn sound ending
in a whistle. One problem was solved.

Halfhyde edged closer, eased his head forward, and looked
into the cave. The moon was shining brightly into it, and it was
shallow enough for everything in it to be seen with total clarity.

There were six young women in grass skirts. They sat in a
circle, motionless and silent. Their breasts were naked, their hair
dark and plaited with wild flowers. It was an uncanny sight.
They sat before the man who was said to be John Frumm, currently asleep and snoring. Halfhyde stared in something like awe
that soon gave way to total astonishment. The figure, short and
fat, was slumped into a replica of a throne, mounted on a dais,
the bare feet resting on a purple cushion that had probably been
filched from a visiting ship. He was wrapped in what appeared
to be a goatskin, a rather smelly one doing duty for a regal cloak
of golden thread, and at his side was a monkey's skull, small
and round, and the thigh bone of either a man or large beast:
the orb and sceptre? Flower petals had been sprinkled liberally
over the goatskin and upon the visible person of John Frumm.
The face was red and even in sleep autocratic; the stomach was
big. A gold-rimmed monocle dangled over it. Beneath the
goatskin peeped very dirty white shorts of a grotesque and too-
familiar length that brought them to just below the knee; and
on the overgrown sandy hair of the head was the gold oak-
leaved peaked cap of a senior British naval officer.

Chapter 6

IT WAS CAPTAIN WATKISS. Fury mingled with amazement. What in God's name was Watkiss doing in the South Pacific anyway, let alone masquerading in the islands as John Frumm? A senior officer so difficult as to be virtually impossible, a man so convinced of his own importance that he would make kings and emperors seem humble by contrast, Captain Watkiss was not entirely a fool and his devotion to the Queen had always been beyond reproach. Halfhyde let out a long breath of exasperation, eased himself away from the rock face and entered the cave boldly with his spear held out in front of his advance.

There were screams from the women and Captain Watkiss woke with a start. "Stop that blasted racket," he snapped, fishing around his goatskin for his monocle, which he thrust angrily into his right eye-socket. He stared at the apparent native. "Who the devil are you, may I ask?"

"I am Halfhyde, sir. Lieutenant Halfhyde, who served under you in—"

"*Halfhyde?* What nonsense; you can't be, you're black."

"Boot polish and mud, sir."

Captain Watkiss peered closer; his jaw dropped. "By God," he said in astonishment. "You *are* Halfhyde. How did you get here?"

"I would like to ask you the same question, sir," Halfhyde said grimly. "As a post captain in Her Majesty's—"

"Hold your tongue!" Watkiss hissed, and indicated the women, who were huddled in a group and staring at the strange native with white patches on his skin. "They have a word or two of English. I'm John Frumm. Kindly remember that, Mr Halfhyde—it's very important, indeed vital to my safety. John Frumm is—"

"I'm aware of the cargo-cults, sir."

"Oh, you are, are you. In that case, you'll appreciate the veneration in which I'm held."

"I think I do, sir, but I must point out that at the moment you're being a considerable embarrassment to His Excellency the Governor and to my commodore, and—"

"Excellency? Commodore?" Watkiss stared. "Where am I precisely, Mr Halfhyde, and what is going on?"

"You are on the South Pacific island of Zanatu, sir, and a rebellion is in progress."

"A *rebellion*? The blasted dagoes, d'you mean?"

Halfhyde nodded. "Yes, sir. They are in revolt against British rule—against the Queen."

"Buggers!"

Halfhyde lifted an eyebrow and gestured towards the huddle of native women. Captain Watkiss was allowing excitement to get the better of his discretion. "Should you not have a care, sir? You said yourself—"

"Oh, balls, Mr Halfhyde, they're much lacking in intelligence. Pray go on."

"Very good, sir. The native rebellion—you are assisting it, passively if not actively. In your capacity as John Frumm the Bountiful, you are being made use of by two men, Dancey and Mulligan—"

"Yes, yes, I know them. They have been most kind. Common

fellows, of course, but respectful I must say. I am well treated." The tone was frosty; and undoubtedly Watkiss appeared well fed. "Pray offer no further impertinence, Mr Halfhyde. I fail to see how I can possibly be assisting the Queen's enemies."

"Through your influence as John Frumm, sir. Backed by you and your inherent guarantee of ease and wealth for the natives, Dancey and Mulligan have suborned the islanders from their loyalties to the Crown, and they have attacked the Residency. I have lost men from my ship's company—lost them to the native spears. That is not all, sir. My commodore—"

"Who is your commodore, Mr Halfhyde?"

"Commodore Bassinghorn, sir. You remember some years ago—"

"Bassinghorn . . . yes, I recall him." Captain Watkiss gave a sniff. "Well, what about him?"

"He is faced by a Russian squadron under Prince Gorsinski, sir."

The monocle dropped to the end of its black silk toggle. Captain Watkiss gaped. "Kindly explain, Mr Halfhyde."

Halfhyde did so, emphasizing the tenseness of the situation and the possibility that war could ensue if a spark should be set to the tinder. Events, he said, were on a knife-edge now that Gorsinski had arrived. With the islanders in a state of armed rebellion, thanks to Dancey and Mulligan, matters were playing into the Russians' hands with a vengeance.

Watkiss asked, "Has Bassinghorn had contact with Prince Gorsinski, Mr Halfhyde?"

"By exchange of signals only, sir. Prince Gorsinski has invited the commodore aboard his flagship, but the commodore has refused."

"So I should damn well think; they're foreigners." Watkiss

pondered, frowning. He drew in the monocle and thrust it back in place. Some flower petals became dislodged; one fluttered up on a slight breeze wafting in from the lagoon. It alighted on the end of Captain Watkiss's nose, and he sneezed violently. His gold-peaked cap went askew and toppled to the ground. Watkiss blew out his cheeks. "Kindly pick it up, Mr Halfhyde—oh, thank you, young woman," he added as one of the grass-skirted maidens retrieved the cap and set it reverently back in place. Watkiss gave her a leer; his attitude towards dago women had always, Halfhyde remembered, been different from his attitude towards dago men.

Halfhyde said sourly, "The cap sits oddly upon the goatskin, sir."

"Never mind that, Mr Halfhyde, the dagoes regard it as my crown." Watkiss drummed his fingers on the arms of his throne; he made a motley monarch. He went on, "What you have told me alters my situation, I fancy. I may be accused of ingratitude but I'm well enough aware of my duty."

"Ingratitude, sir?"

"Yes. You've not yet had the common courtesy to listen to how I got here in the first place, have you?" Watkiss glowered. "I was on long leave from the Fleet, and took the opportunity to visit Australia." Halfhyde recognized "long leave" as an euphemism for half-pay. "I embarked upon a voyage from Brisbane, in a private steam yacht visiting some of the islands, don't you know. The blasted yacht sank—lost with all hands except for me. I drifted about the blasted Pacific in a lifeboat for I don't damn well know how long, Mr Halfhyde! My sufferings . . . but I remained of good heart, we British are like that of course. To cut a long story short, I was found by some dagoes in a canoe and brought ashore. I was wearing my uniform, of course—it does these yacht masters good to have the Queen's uniform aboard their ships and it enabled me to advise authoritatively upon the navigation—and my cap, I believe it was, convinced the dagoes of my importance so far as to make them believe I was John Frumm arrived at last, from out of the sea as he had always been expected to manifest himself, for their special benefit. I was quartered in this cave and provided with servants and everything I desired—"

"Except your freedom, sir?"

"Well, yes. But I found freedom a somewhat disembodied concept, Mr Halfhyde, when I had no idea where in the world I was except that it was upon dry land and I was alive. As I have said, I was well treated and made most welcome. There was a mutual trust, such as I've never experienced with blasted foreigners, don't you know—"

"They trusted you fully, sir?" There was a glint in Halfhyde's eye; he had noticed something: when Watkiss shifted a little his goatskin slid aside and a shaft of moonlight revealed a thick frond of some vegetable matter secured about his stomach, its ends no doubt tied together beneath the throne. Watkiss was griped-in like a sea-boat.

Seeing the direction of Halfhyde's gaze, Watkiss said crossly, "Well, perhaps not. No, not full trust. Or perhaps they simply see me as too valuable to take any risk. I suspect the latter." He paused, then added, "Later on, Dancey and Mulligan turned up and were brought to see me. As I have said, they were kind and respectful and they were *white*. I felt more at home. Possibly you can understand why I used the word ingratitude. I had been given salvation, had been snatched from death's door—"

"By the islanders, sir."

"What?"

"By the islanders. Not by Dancey and Mulligan, who—"

"Ah. Yes, very true," Watkiss said, sounding sage. He lifted a hand and scratched beneath an armpit. "Now, you said something about Dancey and Mulligan suborning the natives from their loyalties, Mr Halfhyde. I think I'm entitled to some explanation?"

"Of course, sir. Dancey and Mulligan are much wanted by the police in Australia. Amongst other things, they are murderers. Some police have been killed." Halfhyde told Captain Watkiss the whole story so far as he knew it.

Watkiss was flabbergasted. "Goodness gracious me, Mr Halfhyde." His jaw sagged, then closed with a snap. "Well, I say again, I know my duty, none better. I am, after all, a—" He broke off, having been about to say he was a post captain of the British Fleet. He glanced at the dusky women. "You know very well what I am, Mr Halfhyde. I have to bear my position in mind, of course." He appeared to reflect a little further; Halfhyde grinned inwardly; as ever, chameleons were amateurs compared with Captain Watkiss. "Well, my dear Halfhyde, it's fortunate you've turned up, most fortunate. I shall accompany you back to your ship without delay, if you'll be so good as to cast off this blasted rope. You'll find other lashings also about my person if you look."

"Indeed, sir?" Halfhyde coughed discreetly. "Your constrictions must have militated against your captor's intentions vis-à-vis your night guard, one would have thought?"

"What the devil d'you mean?" Watkiss asked irritably.

"The women, sir. Their purpose—"

"Hold your tongue and don't be impertinent."

"I apologize, sir. Where are Dancey and Mulligan now?"

Watkiss shrugged. "I've no idea. They come and go. I don't

see much of them; I'm left to the natives. When they do come, the dagoes treat them with deference, almost as they do me."

"Because the Irishmen are regarded as your agents, sir, as coming under the John Frumm aureola. You and they are one in the eyes of the islanders. My original plan was to cut John Frumm out from wherever he was held, and expose him as a fraud—with respect, of course, sir. But now I have come to see the course of the future differently."

"Ah. In what way, may I ask?"

Halfhyde said, "You are no ordinary John Frumm, sir. That's to say, I had expected to find some common seaman, or some trader or such, here in the role of John Frumm. You are not a trader or—"

"Quite." Watkiss nodded vigorously.

"I am glad you agree, sir," Halfhyde said, his tongue in his cheek. "If I may say so, you are an officer of character and decision who knows, as you've said yourself, where his duty lies. Am I not right, sir?"

"Yes, yes. Yes, indeed."

Halfhyde smiled. "Your duty lies here, sir. Your duty is to remain John Frumm for as long as the Queen's service needs you in that capacity."

Watkiss's face reddened dangerously. "Now look here," he said truculently. "You—"

"With respect, sir, my own duty forces me to stress yours. As John Frumm you are much trusted, give or take a rope or two, and much respected. Your word is golden. It carries weight. You can prevent a war, sir, and you can retain Zanatu and its outlying islands for the Empire and the Queen—"

"Oh, balls and bang-me-arse, Mr Halfhyde, how the devil can I do that when I'm tied up here like a—like a—"

"Like John Frumm, sir, whom you truly are in native eyes."
Halfhyde's voice had hardened. "Please listen, sir. You must turn
the islanders' loyalties back towards Her Majesty by use of your
influence. You must tell them that the cargoes will never come
if they continue with the rebellion. You must tell them—"

"But damn it, I can't tell them *anything,* Mr Halfhyde! I haven't
their blasted lingo; I'm not a damn heathen—"

"You've managed thus far, sir."

"Yes, yes," Watkiss said pettishly, "a word or two, a handy
phrase, that's all. Speech has not proved necessary really. Once
the title of John Frumm was attached to me, don't you damn
well see, that was quite enough. The stupid buggers *thought*
themselves into the rest."

Halfhyde said with determination, "To a patriotic officer, sir,
there is always a way of making oneself understood even if only
by mime. You must alter their thoughts and direct them worthily.
You must ensure that the islanders are made aware that Dancey
and Mulligan are wicked men who are acting only for themselves and against the natives." He paused. "You will be invalu-
able to the Fleet as John Frumm if you put your mind wholly
to it, sir."

Yells and curses had followed Halfhyde from the cave as he beat
his retreat into the trees. John Frumm was now far from willing to continue in his role, seeing mortal danger to himself if
matters went awry. Halfhyde had agreed it could come to touch
and go; if when Watkiss turned the tables on them Dancey and
Mulligan managed to persuade the islanders that in fact he had
never been John Frumm at all and it had all been a terrible mistake, then, although the rebellion might well collapse, Captain
Watkiss could find himself turned into a human sacrifice willy-

nilly. He might meet a very ceremonial end indeed. But Halfhyde had not allowed this consideration to alter his determination. He would find a way of rescuing his former captain from his fate, even if it meant the use of the Long Range Squadron's guns; he knew that Bassinghorn would not hesitate to go to the assistance of anyone from the Fleet. In the meantime the Crown was now in possession of a very potent Trojan horse.

In the jungle fringe Halfhyde found his guide: the policeman had waited loyally. The return journey was made more quickly than the outward one, but the dawn was in the sky by the time Halfhyde had reached the western fringe of the trees.

Keeping in cover, he halted. The mob was still before the Residency gates and there was much ground to cover before he could reach the entry in the rear of the stockade. True, there was the available shelter of the trees running round the flanks of the compound, but in daylight the risk was great—too great, perhaps, for him to risk either himself or the policeman. It would be a poor return for the latter's loyalty. Halfhyde made up his mind: he turned aside and headed left, making in the direction of the jetty where the *Talisman* lay. Picking his careful way through the trees with the policeman, he found his thoughts turning back to the cave in the south-east and its much disgruntled occupant. There was a degree of pathos: Watkiss had lost much of his pomposity and fire. Perhaps he was out of practise, having no officers to bawl at and having to mind his Ps and Qs as John Frumm. The natives could be a touchy lot, no doubt, and it would have been much on Watkiss's mind that any non-appearance of cargo within a reasonable time could turn the friendly hands against him. Gone were the imperious days when he strode a quarterdeck or compass platform, gone the days when the lives of midshipmen could be made a living hell of angry comment and wielded canes upon bottoms, gone the days when a first lieutenant could be made to confess in loud tones that he was an incompetent nincompoop, gone the days when the angry stamp of the captain's foot upon the deck could send shivers of fear down the back of a horny-handed chief gunner's mate. With ill luck, Halfhyde thought with a grin, those days could come again all too soon, but for the moment Captain Watkiss was in a state of suppression and it might do him a power of good . . .

Halfhyde and his guide reached the jetty in safety and approached the brow. The quartermaster on watch looked startled for a moment, but was reassured by a word from Halfhyde. Somewhat incongruously saluted aboard, Halfhyde was approached by his first lieutenant.

"Sir."

"Good morning to you, Mr Halliburton. Is all well?"

"Yes, sir."

"I'm glad to hear it. Kindly arrange for this policeman, which is what he is, to be fed and accommodated until after dark." Halfhyde stared round his decks, hands behind his loin cloth. "In the meantime a signal to the commodore, if you please, Mr Halliburton. His steam picket-boat is requested to take me out to the *Port Royal*."

Once again Halfhyde made his way to the commodore's quarters. Bassinghorn stared blankly when Halfhyde reported the identity of John Frumm. "I don't believe it," he said. "You've taken leave of your senses, Halfhyde!"

Halfhyde shook his head. "Far from it, sir. Captain Watkiss, as large as life, crowned with his brass hat and fawned upon by dusky maidens to boot."

Bassinghorn pursed his lips and looked utterly baffled. "How is he?" he asked.

"Muted, sir. A volcano stilled after long eruption." Halfhyde coughed into his hand. "I've left him to it, sir." As briefly as possible, he explained the situation, emphasizing his belief that Watkiss was in a fine position to resolve the whole business. With reservations, Bassinghorn agreed. Watkiss, he said, was not of a persuasive cast of mind and the islanders would not take kindly to raving anger from John Frumm; they would be hurt by being rounded upon by their long awaited benefactor.

"The developments must be carefully watched," Bassinghorn said.

"With a view to the extrication of Captain Watkiss, sir?"

"Amongst other things, yes. It may become necessary to evacuate the Residency if matters fail to go as we hope. I must bear in mind—" Bassinghorn broke off as a knock came at his day-cabin door. The officer of the watch appeared, the frog-ends of his black patent-leather sword-belt dangling at his left side. "Yes, Mr Pearson, what is it?"

"A pinnace is coming off from the Russian flagship, sir, with the admiral embarked."

Bassinghorn glared. "Is it indeed?" He appeared suddenly irresolute. "Damn the fellow, I can scarcely turn him away, a fact he'll be well aware of—but I've a damn good mind to do so! The hour is unconscionably early for a call in any case. What do you think, Halfhyde?"

"I'd allow him aboard, sir. I think there has to be contact. But as for me, I propose to make myself very scarce!"

Chapter 7

THE TWO IRISHMEN, Dancey and Mulligan, sat in a native hut built of mud and vegetable matter at the western extremity of Zanatu. A stout tarpaulin had been laid on the earth floor and upon it Dancey was cleaning and oiling a stripped-down Maxim gun, British Army pattern. This, along with sundry other weapons and ammunition, had been stolen from an ambushed ordnance train running on the Main Trunk Line of the Queensland Central Railway from Longreach to Rockhampton, smuggled out of Australia via an inlet behind the Great Barrier Reef, and brought in unmarked crates to Zanatu by a trading vessel under sail. Some killing had been necessary along the way, but neither Dancey nor Mulligan were inexperienced as murderers. Each had a long list of crimes committed in the Australian colonies and in Ireland as well. They would never willingly set foot in either Ireland or Australia again. Since their arrival in Zanatu, their considerable armoury had been further supplemented by the revolvers on the persons of the police inspector and his constables from Sydney.

Working away at the Maxim, Dancey said, "That John Frumm."

"What about him?"

"Suppose the British Navy finds him, eh?"

Mulligan jeered. "They'll never!"

"Just suppose they did. What will they do?" Dancey leaned

forward. "I'll tell you, mate: they'll hook him away, that's for sure. Then what about us, eh?"

"One of us takes over."

"Becomes John Frumm?"

"Right."

"Never! That wouldn't wash. That bloke, he's John Frumm to the bloody blacks and you won't convince the buggers different, not now." Dancey, mouth set like a rat-trap, wiped an oily rag over a piece of gunmetal, eyes narrowed. He looked like a black rat, small and wiry and evil, with dark hair, the most dangerous species. "All right, we're his agents, his mates—they believe that, sure. But we can't take his place, see? He's the flaming fount . . . if he dries up, so do we."

Mulligan nodded, but said with confidence, "The Britishers won't find him, don't worry."

"I do worry," Dancey said viciously. "Bloody British, poking about like they always do, one day they'll stumble on him. Now there's the Russians too. This thing's got big."

Mulligan grinned. "Want to get out, do you, Dancey?"

"No. Here we are, here we stick. We just have to ride it for a while, that's all. Wait long enough and both sets of ships will steam away. It's the in-between, see. I tell you something."

"What?"

"John Frumm's due for a shift of bloody residence and the sooner the better." Dancey finished his labours on the Maxim, working swiftly and expertly: there had been a time when he had served in the British Army, in the Leinster Regiment, his service terminating in desertion following upon a flogging for theft. "We'll go and get him as soon as this lot's stowed away down below. He'll live with *us* for a while, where we can keep a personal eye on him, see?"

•   •   •

"Young woman! You there—that one. Oh, for heaven's sake, why don't you *pay attention?*"

Captain Watkiss was in a quandary: communication with his maidens was extremely difficult, had been all along, though over the weeks he had picked up a word or two of their dago lingo and they had acquired a few useful words of the Queen's English. It didn't amount to much and now there was that desperate need to get something across about loyalty and the Queen. Halfhyde had been perfectly right, although Captain Watkiss was still furious at being abandoned by one of his former officers. That was unforgivable; yet it was perhaps inevitable. In the meantime Captain Watkiss intended to do his duty to Her Majesty, to make the blasted dagoes understand that nothing in the way of cargo would come their way unless they withdrew from rebellious acts.

He had succeeded in attracting the young woman's attention now. He had chosen the prettiest, who appeared also to be the most intelligent and the one with the best command of English; she approached and knelt daintily. Watkiss sighed and said, "Thank God! Now, there's a matter of urgency. Of importance. I would like to see the headman."

"Men come soon, John Frumm."

"Yes, I know," Watkiss snapped. The guard relief for the women was due, it being daylight now. "That was not my point. Not men—*headman,* singular."

"Men come soon," the girl repeated, looking nervous. John Frumm might well prove bountiful in due course, but he was an angry benefactor. She said it again for good measure, to propitiate her god. "Men come soon."

Captain Watkiss breathed hard down his nose. "Oh, damn

and blast you, woman! Headman, headman, headman! I don't
know why it's always my lot to suffer blasted fools!"

"Men come soon." The young woman was close to tears. She
would never be forgiven for upsetting John Frumm. "Men—"

"Oh, hold your tongue."

"—come soon."

"God give me strength." Watkiss heaved his thick body
around beneath the goatskin. He was sweating freely; soon it
would be worse as the sun rose higher, but fortunately it was
relatively cool in the cave, shallow though it was. He was pro-
tected from the direct rays of the sun, which was lucky, otherwise by this time he would be as black as a dago himself. He
lifted his fists in the air, clenched from his dreadful frustration
at not being able to make himself understood at a time of great
importance for the Empire. Until now it hadn't mattered so very
much; at first beside himself with rage and offended dignity at
his incarceration—after feelings of gratitude for deliverance from
the deep had receded—Captain Watkiss had, after a while, grown
comatose in his acquiescence in his role as John Frumm, which
was a comfortable one and obviously important. He liked deference—always had; the Navy had accustomed him to it once
he had got through his midshipman's time. The island air was
balmy, the food good, and although of course he didn't believe
all the rubbish about cargo-cults, he had recognized a large
degree of good fortune: it was all very much better than being
devoured by sharks, which might have been his lot in the end.

Then Halfhyde had come and Watkiss's eyes had been opened
very sharply. The Fleet had come back to him with all its majesty,
all its great ships and guns and quarterdecks, and all of a sudden he couldn't wait to be free to rejoin. Zanatu, as the island

appeared to be named according to Halfhyde—Watkiss had in fact never heard of it before—had become inimical and his role as John Frumm a millstone about his neck. Queen Victoria beckoned from Windsor Castle, or from Balmoral in far distant Scotland, wherever she happened to be at the time.

How he could ever have forgotten . . .

He saw a shadow against the sun: a person had approached the mouth of his cave. Halfhyde again? No. It was the man Dancey, and Mulligan was with him.

"Good morning," Captain Watkiss said. He said it politely; he was not supposed to be aware of the truth about the Irishmen and he must play his new role cautiously.

"Good for some," Dancey said, advancing into the cave.

Watkiss didn't care for the tone. "I beg your pardon?"

"Good for some, but not for you, John bloody Frumm."

"I don't understand."

"You will." Dancey bent and fiddled about beneath the throne. Captain Watkiss felt his bonds slacken away. "Get up," Dancey said.

"Why should I?"

"Because I say so."

"I call that rude."

"Call it what you bloody like. Get up!"

Watkiss seethed, but with some difficulty got up—he was stiff, despite daily exercise. As he came clear of his throne, he felt the hard nudge of a revolver in his back. He was quite incredulous: Dancey and Mulligan had changed their tune with a vengeance and that fact alone proved that Halfhyde had spoken nothing but the truth. The Irishmen had no doubt become rattled by the presence of Bassinghorn's squadron.

Dancey said, "Move."

"I shall do no such thing. I refuse to be given orders by low fellows of your class."

There was a pause. Then Dancey said, "Now listen. You're still John Frumm to the bloody natives. That doesn't change. The women haven't seen the gun. I'm not going to smash your face in with them looking on. But if you don't do as I say from now on, then God help you just as soon as we're alone. One thing more. If you decide to play up now, I'll shoot you in the bloody legs so you can't run, and then I'll have to kill the women. All of them. Make up your mind."

Watkiss gave a gasp. The gloves were right off now. The women had been good to him; it wouldn't be cowardice on his part to protect their lives in return. He said offendedly, "Oh, very well. Where do you want me to go?"

"You'll see. Just keep close behind Mulligan, who'll lead the way."

Captain Watkiss found his heart beating rather fast as he left the cave between the two Irishmen. *Irishmen* . . . he might have known! A rebellious lot at the best of times, and untrustworthy. Look at that fellow Wolfe Tone, and Napper Tandy too—right back into history, the Irish had been quite impossible. In recent times Parnell had been involved in a divorce, a terrible thing. Not English at all. Blasted bog-trotters. Colonists were a rum bunch too: Captain Watkiss had found he hadn't liked Australia at all; there was a lack of deference for his position as a post captain.

He moved out and because Dancey and Mulligan walked quickly he had a job to keep up and kept coming into contact with Dancey's revolver. He scuttled along, panting, a red-faced John Frumm shifting berth, clutching at his crown and monkey-skull and trailing his goatskin.

• • •

On board the *Port Royal* Halfhyde was concealed in Bassinghorn's sleeping-cabin, which led off the day-cabin. With luck he would be able to hear the conversation at first hand without having to await Bassinghorn's summary afterwards. As the Russian pinnace made its approach, Halfhyde heard the bugles of the Royal Marine Light Infantry sounding the still. The bugles were followed by the fifes and drums playing the general salute, after which the boatswain's calls were heard piping Admiral Prince Gorsinski aboard.

After a while footsteps entered the day-cabin. Halfhyde heard Bassinghorn sending his steward for gin; there was some polite chit-chat, followed by silence as the gin was poured.

Gorsinski's harsh, autocratic voice was next heard in a toast: "His Imperial Majesty the Czar of all the Russias."

"And Her Majesty Queen Victoria," Bassinghorn said.

There was a brief but telling hesitation. "Ah, yes. And Her Majesty Queen Victoria. More gin, please. You have no vodka?"

"No vodka, Your Highness."

"Ah. Then the gin."

There was another pause. Bassinghorn broke it by coming straight to the point: he was no diplomat. "Tell me, Your Highness," he said abruptly. "What are your ships doing here in British waters?"

"British waters, Commodore?"

"British waters," Bassinghorn repeated firmly. "Zanatu and its group of islands are the property of the Crown, and are thus British sovereign territory—"

"Currently in revolt."

"That's as may be, Your Highness. You still need permission to lie off, and I've received no notification from the Admiralty that you have such permission." Bassinghorn hesitated. "Of course, if permission has been granted you since I left my last port, then I must apologize."

Gorsinski laughed. "Permission, Commodore? I represent my Czar, and he does not seek *permission* for his ships to sail the seas! Does Queen Victoria lay claim to all the waters of the Pacific Ocean?"

Bassinghorn didn't answer straight away; Halfhyde could sense his self-anger at having over-reached himself. Gorsinski had made a perfectly valid point. Nevertheless Bassinghorn's basic point was equally valid in the sense that no one but a fool could doubt that the Russian squadron was present for no purpose welcome to the British; but he could have put it better. A moment later he tried, gruffly, to do so. He said, "I must ask you what your interest is in Zanatu, Your Highness."

A laugh floated through to the sleeping-cabin. "My interest is my Czar's interest, Commodore."

"That doesn't answer my question."

"No? Then I will say this: my Czar is a humane man and where he sees oppression he hastens to help to put matters right."

"I think my government can manage very well without his assistance, Your Highness." To himself in the sleeping-cabin, Halfhyde registered sardonic agreement: Czar Nicholas might well be a kindly man, but there was any amount of oppression to occupy his attention in his own country.

"Mediation," Gorsinski said, "is always helpful."

"But interference is not," Bassinghorn said with a snap in his voice. "I'm sorry, Your Highness, but you compel me to be forthright. I am here under orders from—"

"From Queen Victoria, to put down the rebellion by force of your guns, I think?"

"Not from Her Majesty, in point of fact—from the Admiralty."

"It is the same thing," Gorsinski said off-handedly.

"Your pardon, it is not. And I have no specific orders to use my guns. I am here to render background assistance to Sir Wilbraham Carse, the Governor. In effect, I am the mediator, Your Highness."

"I see. As always, the British are so good at the use of euphemisms," Gorsinski said in a sneering tone. "As matters stand, I shall consider myself and my ships as guarantors that there will be no slaughter of innocent natives—I say no more than that. It is up to you. You will have observed my guns. They are many, and they are heavy. I am a peaceful man, but—"

"An ambitious one, Your Highness! I believe your purpose here to be to make use of the islanders' rebellion to extend your own Empire, to—"

"No. I have been given no orders in that direction." There was a small sound as of Gorsinski setting down his glass somewhat hard upon a table. "I am here for no more reason than I have already given, Commodore. Yet there is one thing I confess an interest in."

"And that is?"

Gorsinski said, "In the Pacific, as I am sure you know, rumour spreads with the speed of lightning. It is like the dubious joke, that is for the first time told one day in Moscow and the next is heard in Siberia. You understand? Now there is a rumour in many islands to the north that John Frumm has come to Zanatu. You will be aware of this?"

"Yes," Bassinghorn answered.

"I am interested in John Frumm. He is a valuable person. He who possesses John Frumm holds power in many islands, many archipelagos." There was another pause. "John Frumm may be the means of avoiding any unpleasantness, Commodore . . ."

Shortly after, Prince Gorsinski was heard to leave the commodore's quarters and the sounds of international goodwill and politeness were flamboyantly repeated.

Bassinghorn came down again to his day-cabin after saluting his visitor away and called for Halfhyde. "You heard all that?" he asked, as Halfhyde emerged.

"Most of it, I believe, sir. Prince Gorsinski wasn't over specific at the end, but I believe I got the drift."

"Which is?"

"That Captain Watkiss is standing upon very thin ice, sir."

Bassinghorn gave a hard, humourless laugh. "Yes, you're right, Halfhyde. It's a case of a Frumm for a farewell . . . the Russians will steam away if John Frumm can be found and delivered to them. Gorsinski sees John Frumm as worth more than Zanatu, it seems. As for me, I take his point: a roving John Frumm, promising all the earth's cargoes if a Russian presence is admitted first, willingly and without bloodshed, could give the whole Pacific to the Czar! Not a voice could legitimately be raised in protest if the inhabitants of uncolonized islands asked for the Russians to move in—do you see, Halfhyde?"

"Yes, sir, indeed I do. I see immense danger to British interests. It's entirely feasible, given the inbred superstitions of all the Pacific islanders." Halfhyde paused. "Captain Watkiss has become a stick of dynamite, sir, presented directly at the Queen's throat!"

"And must be prevented from blowing himself up." Bassinghorn paced the day-cabin. "He should be brought aboard my squadron, Halfhyde, without delay. He's too dangerous now to leave to the islanders. The Russians may try to cut him out."

"I'm not sure I agree entirely, sir. Gorsinski is in no position to land men without us knowing—"

"After dark?"

Halfhyde said, "We can institute patrols, sir."

"Possibly. You're suggesting that Captain Watkiss can still act to quell the rebellion?"

"I believe so, sir. In the current situation, that's almost as vital as protecting John Frumm from the Russians. I would suggest, sir, that at least we give him more time to see what he can do."

"And we, in the meantime?"

"I think we must play a waiting game, sir—and ensure that no men are landed from the Russian squadron. And I'd suggest one thing more: that the time has come for the Governor to be prevented from entertaining Prince Gorsinski in the Residency, which I believe he has half a mind to do."

Bassinghorn smiled. "I have changed his mind for him, Halfhyde. I made a signal soon after dawn, since I expected he might have ideas of protocol. And somehow I doubt if Gorsinski will be much surprised when no invitation comes to him! As for you, what do you propose to do now?"

"I shall go back ashore, sir, if you'll provide a boat. My ship is in good hands, and I shall make the Residency my head-quarters for the time being."

"And keep an eye lifting on John Frumm?"

"So far as possible, sir, yes. It wouldn't do for me to be seen in company with him—I was lucky last night. I might not be so next time." Halfhyde smiled. "He'll need no more prompting, sir. I spoke of the Queen, and Her Majesty's dependence upon him. There is no one in the Fleet who has more reverence for the Monarch than John Frumm."

Halfhyde was taken back into the lagoon. By now the heat of the day had struck full; the blue water shimmered under a brassy sky and bare skin burned. There was not the faintest breeze to stir the palms. Behind Halfhyde as he headed inshore the bugles blared from the Long Range Squadron, sending the ships' companies to Divisions and inspection by their officers. Looking back, Halfhyde watched the hundreds of men doubling on bare feet to fall in, saw the padre of the *Port Royal* walking with bent head and flowing surplice to the rostrum rigged for him to conduct morning prayers. Before the steam picket-boat had reached the entry to the lagoon the assembled all-male voices could be heard thundering out the first hymn. Halfhyde listened to the familiar words:

Onward, Christian soldiers,
Marching as to war,
With the Cross of Jesus
Going on before . . .

It was being sung with some special fervour, almost with relish in the word "war." The British Fleet had never shrunk from fighting and the tars were as bold as they had been in Nelson's day, and undoubtedly rumour would have been rife along the mess decks. Bassinghorn, with his high responsibilities and his knowledge of intrigue in privileged places, his awareness of royal relationships by blood and marriage, would be less keen than his seamen for war to take place. If any mistake were made, heads could roll: Bassinghorn's would be the first, then Sir Wilbraham's. Yet Bassinghorn was not disposed to flinch: before Halfhyde had left his quarters the commodore had faced him with a formidable expression and passed orders that he was to look to his remaining torpedo-tube; this was to be in all respects ready for use if required at short notice. He had added nothing further; but Halfhyde had taken the point. Prince Gorsinski had heavy ships and heavy guns, but he had no torpedoes. The *Talisman* was highly manoeuvrable, and could slip beneath the great gun-batteries, with luck remaining unhit until she had loosed off her shards of death and destruction.

On arrival in the Residency Halfhyde was met by Mr Stallybrass, whom he took aside for a quiet word. He passed the commodore's orders. He said, "I told the commodore I had a first-class torpedo-gunner, Mr Stallybrass. The torpedoes, I said, are always ready, and in need of no urging from myself."

"That's right, sir. When do we go back aboard, sir?"

Halfhyde smiled down at the portly, eager warrant officer; Stallybrass seemed only half alive when away from his beloved torpedo-tubes: he was virtually married to them. "As soon as circumstances permit, Mr Stallybrass, I promise you. For now we must await activity from John Frumm—or Prince Gorsinski!"

The walk in front of Dancey's revolver had been a long one and Captain Watkiss's feet were sore. Naval officers were more accustomed to flat, holystoned decks than to twisted jungly roots, jagged rock, and sand into which the feet sank deep and had to be dragged up again. And it was so hot; Captain Watkiss moved in a bath of sweat, complainingly.

"I can't go on much longer."

"You'll do as you're bloody told, mate."

"I'm no longer young, blast you! I'm out of condition."

There was an unfeeling laugh. "Too much sitting on that bloody throne. Lucky you haven't got piles."

Watkiss simmered with anger as well as the stifling heat: the gibe was not worth responding to, such a common thing to say. He felt hurt at the sudden tremendous change in the two Irishmen's attitudes towards him; and a core of cold hatred had developed in him very quickly towards men who had pulled the wool over his eyes in so dastardly a fashion. What Halfhyde had said about the men's dreadful record of murder and pillage had been a great shock. But that sudden change: it must be due to fear now that Bassinghorn had arrived, and fear in Dancey and Mulligan gave hope to Captain Watkiss. His ordeal must come to an end soon, it stood to reason, Bassinghorn would do something as soon as he knew. In the meantime he was being prevented from carrying out his duty to reverse the native rebellion; it was unlikely that he would be put in contact with the headman now. Something was telling him that very conclusively. John Frumm was no longer the honoured figure that he had been until this morning.

The walk ended at last. It ended unpropitiously for Captain Watkiss. First they came to an isolated native mud hut, an appalling-looking place, then they came to something very much worse: a hole in the ground, revealed when Mulligan rolled a large boulder aside. Captain Watkiss was pushed towards it by Dancey's revolver. The hole had an inhabited look; a roughly-constructed wooden ladder led down into pitch darkness but Mulligan went ahead, down the ladder, and then light and smoke came up. Mulligan had ignited a torch and Captain Watkiss was able to see furnishings of a sort: piles of dried and chopped undergrowth, probably for use as bedding, and a table and chairs roughly made from indigenous wood like the ladder. This, presumably, was where Dancey and Mulligan lived and it would obviously be next to impossible for anyone to find. The future once again looked bleak.

"Down the ladder," Dancey said behind him

Watkiss shivered despite the terrible heat. Gingerly he stretched out a foot to the ladder. It held, but shifted a little at its bottom end when Watkiss's full weight came on it. However, he was a seaman well accustomed to ladders and he made the descent in safety, only to be almost asphyxiated by the smoke from the torch. He spluttered and coughed.

"Shut up," Mulligan said.

"I can't breathe."

"Yes, you can if you bloody try," Dancey said, still from behind. "*We* can. We've breathed it ever since the bloody cops came from Sydney."

The Sydney police . . . killed by these two! Captain Watkiss felt a shake in his limbs and dropped heavily to one of the piles of undergrowth. As he made contact, something slithered from beneath his bottom and scuttled away, making a rasping sound. Trying to follow the creature's movement so as to be sure of moving aside should it come back, Watkiss saw the reflection of the torch from metal. Guns . . . the stripped-down parts of a Maxim, many rifles, also revolvers, plus a box of grenades and quantities of ammunition. The place was an arsenal as well as a home. They wouldn't be able to leave him there alone, that was certain. But they had thought of that. Dancey ferreted about behind the boxed ammunition and produced two pairs of handcuffs. He jingled them in Watkiss's face.

"Courtesy of Sydney peelers," he said. "Keys and all." He approached Watkiss and snapped one pair round his ankles while Mulligan held the revolver, and another on his wrists, first drawing them round to his back. Watkiss lay trussed like a chicken ready for the oven. "You muck about with the armoury," Dancey said threateningly, as though he could, other than by rolling on to it, "and all you'll do is blow yourself into frag-ments." Both men moved to the ladder. "We'll be back."

"I shan't be able to breathe," Watkiss said, "if you put that boulder in place."

"Yes, you will. Enough air comes round the sides. It'll be stuffy, but you'll live." There was a laugh. "Don't worry, we still need you."

They went up the ladder. The boulder was rolled over the hole, settling with a nasty thud. They had extinguished the torch—thank God, considering the ammunition—and the dark-ness was total except for thin chinks of sun striking through from the boulder's sides. There was utter silence, blank and frightening. Captain Watkiss shook more than ever and found that he was quite unable to shift his thoughts to the clean blue sea and the dignity of a post captain's quarters afloat.

Chapter 8

"CAPTAIN, SIR!"

It was the torpedo-gunner's voice; Halfhyde, who had been conferring with the Governor and the ADC, swung round, "Yes, Mr Stallybrass, what is it?"

"Attack, sir! The buggers are massed by the gate and about to break their way in, sir."

Halfhyde ran across the room to a tall window. The islanders were there in force, many hundreds of them, but they were maintaining a curious silence which was of itself threatening. They were well armed, not only with their bows-and-arrows and spears but also with rifles of British pattern—Lee Enfields as used by the army. Halfhyde turned from the window, calling for the landing-parties to stand to. He ran into the central hall of the Residency as the men began to muster. Then the silence broke. The keening started, much louder than had been heard before. As the sound increased, the islanders moved back in a surging wave, away from the gate towards the jungle, leaving one man who was seen with a huge axe lifted high—again a prize taken from army stores, an axe such as was carried on parade by a battalion's pioneer sergeant. The axe came down on the gate before the defenders could react, and the woodwork shuddered to the impact and split. Before a second blow could fall the native spun in a circle and dropped, taken in the chest by a bullet as Halfhyde gave the order to open fire. The men of the landing-party fanned out, crouched low behind their rifles, and sent volley after volley crashing into the islanders' ranks. Halfhyde turned away, calling for his signalman.

"Here, sir!"

"To the roof, Umpleby. From *Talisman* to the commodore by semaphore: *request immediate assistance at the Residency. Am under heavy attack.*"

"Aye, aye, sir!" Umpleby saluted and went at the double to the Residency roof. Halfhyde went back smartly to the battle that was now raging at the perimeter stockade as the natives returned the naval fire. Bullets smacked viciously off the walls of the Residency, though too many of them found their human targets, and the British fire dwindled. Then the whole mass of the attackers came forward from the position by the trees that they had initially retreated to. They came fast as the wind and flung their bodies full against the stout wood of the stockade. It lurched and creaked alarmingly. Then again, and again. Halfhyde stared grimly: if Bassinghorn's reinforcements didn't come very soon, there might well be no one left alive.

Prince Gorsinski, having bathed refreshingly in cold water, fresh water such as was denied his ship's company on account of its scarcity, was being powdered and cologned by his servant when a loud knock came at his day-cabin door and the officer of the watch was heard calling for him.

"What is it?"

"The island, Your Highness." The officer of the watch remained invisible beyond the closed door of the bathroom: His Highness could not be looked upon naked. "There is the sound of rifle fire, and the—"

"Fire, where?"

"I believe from the British Residency, Your Highness."

"I see." Gorsinski, impatiently gesturing his servant to continue his ministrations, submitted to a comb being drawn through his beard. "Go back to the quarterdeck, and keep me informed."

"Yes, Your Highness." There was a pause. "You have other orders, Your Highness?"

"If I had," Gorsinski said coldly, "be sure I would have given them and would have had your wretched hide had they not been obeyed instantly."

"Yes, Your Highness."

"I have no orders. I propose to allow the British to be drawn into battle without interference from me—at this stage. With luck they will be slaughtered. Now obey my orders and go back to the quarterdeck immediately." Gorsinski rounded upon his servant, who cringed. "The cologne all over, you fool, my whole body. I do not propose to stink like you and the other vermin on my mess decks." He stared at his reflection in the looking-glass, eyes slanted disdainfully down the thin, aristocratic nose. The beard needed trimming; he indicated the fact. "The scissors, damn you, and have a care to wield them not too little, not too much." The beautification continued and was not hurried. Within the next ten minutes the officer of the watch came down again with a report that the British cruisers were sending boats inshore.

Umpleby came down from the roof at the rush. "Boats coming in now, sir!" he shouted as he saw Halfhyde.

"How many?"

"Six cutters and whalers, sir, and a steam pinnace."

"Good!" Halfhyde turned back to the compound, now strewn with dead and wounded, both British and native. A breach had

been made in the perimeter stockade but the fence as a whole
was bearing up yet, and the narrowness of the breach rendered
the native assault more or less containable. Bullets were pumped
across and not many of the islanders survived to penetrate far.
By Halfhyde's order the Governor was keeping well out of it; he
was in his study doing his best to comfort his wife. When cheering was heard from the compound, Sir Wilbraham took heart.
He left the study and went into the hall. There was a good deal
of rifle fire coming from outside the stockade, from the right of
the native mass, which was starting to turn away for the trees.
Soon after this the leading files of the relief force came into view,
marching steadfastly for the compound in duck suits and gaiters,
shoulder to shoulder with their rifles and leather bandoliers of
cartridges. In charge was the gunnery lieutenant from the *Port
Royal* flourishing a sword as he marched in the lead of some
ninety to a hundred seamen and stokers, with two gunner's
mates bringing up the rear. There was more cheering as the men
were deployed to right and left, and brought up their rifles to
cover the retreating mob. A volley of hastening shots was sent
across. After this the seamen held their fire, waiting in their
crouched positions, fingers round the trigger-guards. Their very
presence seemed to be enough: the islanders melted into the
trees and no further attack developed. Halfhyde took stock of
the situation: of his original landing-parties, twelve more men
lay dead on the compound to be added to those already in the
burial ground; and eighteen others were wounded in varying
degrees. It was a sad toll. He was about to send his signalman
to the roof once more, to report to the commodore that for the
time being the situation was being held, when the gunnery lieutenant marched up to him.

"Lieutenant Halfhyde, I think?"

"Yes."

"My name's Foster-Martin. I'm ordered by the commodore to evacuate the Residency as soon as the situation permits."

"I see. And His Excellency? Suppose he doesn't agree?"

"I'm under orders to bring him off nevertheless. The commodore's concerned for his safety, and for Lady Carse and the British staff. It's understood that there are no other white people on the island—other than the two Irishmen, and—"

"And John Frumm."

Foster-Martin nodded. "That's right. He's to be brought off too, but the evacuation is not to be delayed pending his being apprehended. Your orders from the commodore are that you return aboard your ship with your men. I shall see to the evacuation, and it will be up to you to get hold of John Frumm and then have him sent off to the *Port Royal*."

Before the withdrawal took place, the burials were conducted: this was preferable to taking the bodies out to the cruisers for a sea committal. With the ships likely to remain on station, the superstitious seaman's mind would not allow the ships' companies to rest easy with the corpses of their comrades surging about below them. Sir Wilbraham Carse was unexpectedly acquiescent in accepting Bassinghorn's order to leave the island. His world had already broken about his ears and he was concerned for his wife; Halfhyde comforted him so far as he could with an assurance that he would be allowed back once the revolt had been finally put down with the arrest of the Irishmen who had caused it. The Long Range Squadron, he said, would not leave the islands until that had been achieved. The Governor nodded listlessly but said that he would never come back to the aban-doned Residency itself: the moment he and his entourage moved out, it was likely to be sacked by the mob. Halfhyde, who had no orders from Bassinghorn to act in its defence, had no reas-suring words to offer on that score. The Residency, after all, was only a building; Bassinghorn was right to put life first.

They moved out, strongly guarded by the armed parties marching to either flank. The policemen, the refugee families, and the Residency servants left with His Excellency: had they remained behind, there was little doubt that they would have been slaughtered by the rebels. Halfhyde accompanied the evac-uation as far as the jetty, where he detached with his own men for the *Talisman*. Piped aboard to be greeted by Mr Halliburton standing at the salute by the brow, he watched as the boats headed out of the lagoon towards the open sea and the cruis-ers. There was a feeling of defeat as the Residency staff moved away over the blue water with its collective tail between its legs. Defeat had to be temporary. Dancey and Mulligan must not be allowed to get away with *lèse-majesté*.

Halfhyde turned to his first lieutenant. "The casualties," he said. The ship would be short-handed now; all the wounded had been sent away with the evacuation party for attention aboard the *Port Royal* with its doctors and sick berth. "See to it that the torpedo-coxswain draws up a fresh Watch and Quarter Bill at once, Mr Halliburton. We may be required to move out to sea at short notice and we must be ready."

"Aye, aye, sir."

"But first there is John Frumm. I shall wait till after dark, then I shall land and bring him back aboard."

"You, sir?"

Halfhyde nodded. "I know where John Frumm is. No one else knows, therefore the task must be mine." He turned away and went below to his cabin, as small as his bridge, not to be compared with the luxury of Bassinghorn's quarters. In the island's heat he found it claustrophobic and lingered only long enough to call for his servant to bring a clean uniform and a tub of bathwater. Washed and shaved he returned to the upper deck and sat in a chair beneath the quarterdeck awning. He sat alone; there was an isolation in command for a lieutenant as for a post captain. Intimacy with one's subordinates was not encouraged in the Fleet, since familiarity tended to reduce awe and was thus bad for discipline, and the efficiency of the Navy depended upon its iron-hard discipline and the instilled belief that the captain was infallible. Halfhyde shifted restlessly in the still, close air. He knew he was not infallible; he was as capable of making a bad decision as was anyone else, and he believed now that he had made a wrong decision in regard to John Frumm who, as Captain Watkiss, had never entertained any doubts whatsoever as to his own infallibility. Captain Watkiss had always had the immense psychological advantage, to himself at any rate, of knowing for certain that he was right; a post captain could not be wrong. To Watkiss, that notion had the force of an axiom. Perhaps this time he *had* been right: he should have been removed once found, and taken aboard the *Port Royal* to be a confounded nuisance to Bassinghorn. Now, because of Gorsinski, he had become a danger to the squadron, such that could lead to a clash of arms with the Russians . . .

Halfhyde got to his feet and paced the quarterdeck, frowning in anxiety. He had not been certain he knew the land route back to the cave; he could have kept his policeman guide instead of sending him with the evacuation, but had preferred a different approach—by water. That would be much faster, given a good whaler's crew, but there were disadvantages in that a boat would stand out to watching eyes as it crossed the lagoon and the bay—and so far as that went, a large body of men pressing through the jungle could equally be seen or heard, all of which he had borne in mind on his first journey to the cave. It was his ability to take an armed party with him by water that had weighed most in his decision, but he was not unaware of the dangers.

He paced on, wishing the day away so that the chafe of inaction could give place to the start of the night's work. The vacuum of waiting brought too many doubts and fears. However, the natural processes of time could never be hurried; and at last, after a splendid, many-coloured sunset that had rendered the sky like fire rolling over the South Pacific, the sun was nicely down. Halfhyde sent for his first lieutenant, and Mr Halliburton came aft to the quarterdeck.

"Mr Halliburton, you may call away the whaler—but quietly. Word of mouth, not the pipe."

"Aye, aye, sir."

"And muster the landing-party as detailed, if you please."

The first lieutenant saluted and turned away to pass the orders. Halfhyde stared around at the dark water and at the darker loom of the land with its close-set jungle. God alone could tell what lurked in there, how many eyes might be watching. That was a chance that must be taken. As Halfhyde looked he saw what at first he imagined might be the last spark of the sunset, a small glow to the north of the jetty, a reddish yellow such as had been one of the constituent colours recently in the sky. But a moment's thought told him this was unlikely. He stiffened in anger, his face set and long jaw out-thrust. The Residency: torches had been set to it and were already taking a hold of furnishings and woodwork. The glow increased with surprising speed and soon flames were shooting into the sky and the distant crackling could be clearly heard.

Halliburton approached at the double.

"Sir, the Residency—"

"Yes, Mr Halliburton, and there is nothing to be done about it."

"But—"

"No buts, Mr Halliburton, we are powerless—unless you imagine the wash-deck hoses can be run out to such a distance!"

"No, sir."

"Then we must leave it to burn, and I fancy it's a case of an ill wind that blows no one any good. If luck's on our side, Mr Halliburton, the Residency will act as a magnet to the islanders who'll not want to miss a good bonfire! Is the whaler ready?"

"It'll be alongside in half a minute, sir."

Halfhyde nodded. There was a rattle of rifle-slings and other equipment as the landing-party mustered alongside the starboard torpedo-tube under the gunner's mate. Voices were being kept low as though each man feared to disturb the evil that might be listening from the jungle's cover. True to Halliburton's promise, the whaler came alongside the quarterdeck ladder within the half minute and without delay the landing-party was marched along to embark.

Halfhyde followed them down into the boat then lifted a hand to the first lieutenant. Mr Halliburton called down to the coxswain to carry on. Boathooks bore the whaler off the ship's side and she drifted clear. To the coxswain's low-voiced order,

the oars took the water and flung spray glinted white beneath
a moon that was already climbing the sky. The whaler, with
Halfhyde in the stern-sheets, clad like all the others in a blue
uniform the better to remain unseen once ashore, moved under
a strong, steady pull past an arm of the land to the south of the
jetty and headed towards the next arm, the one that enclosed
the nearer side of the bay.

On the shore, the sand glowed silvery white in the moon's
beams. There was no sign of anything moving there. Beyond the
sand the jungle rose dark and menacing; beyond again the flames
from the burning Residency shot into the sky, baleful fingers that
tipped the trees with angry red. Halfhyde spared a thought for
the feelings of Sir Wilbraham and Lady Carse, perhaps watching from the deck of the *Port Royal*. Gone already the work of
years, now going, for all Halfhyde knew, a lifetime's collection
of furniture and trinkets, all at the whim of two criminals who
cared not a jot for the islanders' welfare. Halfhyde fingered his
holstered revolver and thought grim and bloody thoughts. If he
got Dancey or Mulligan in his sights, he might well pre-empt
the attentions of the hangman.

The whaler sped on through the night. Halfhyde brought out
his watch: there was enough moon for him to see its face. They
were making good time. The bay was not far off now. With luck
he would soon have the *Talisman* out to sea: there was no point
in his remaining alongside the jetty once John Frumm was safe
aboard, and his intention was to leave the lagoon and take his
prize out to the *Port Royal* himself and then await Bassinghorn's
further orders.

The whaler had rounded the arm of the land and was making across the bay when the coxswain called softly, "Captain, sir!"

"Yes?"

"A ship, sir, a cruiser . . . outside the reef, sir, steaming west-wards."

With an oath, Halfhyde turned to look. He doubted if Bassinghorn would be ordering way upon his ships. He was right. The cruiser, stark beneath the moon, was neither the *Port Royal* nor the *Plantagenet.* She was without doubt a Russian, and for a certainty it would not be long before the whaler was seen if it hadn't been already. The Russian might be intending to put parties ashore, taking the burning Residency as a sign that the British were on the run and that the island was wide open to their own purposes: principally, perhaps, those purposes would be John Frumm. Halfhyde, however, had the advantage yet: the Russians had to get a boat into the lagoon. He said, "Backs into it, Coxswain. All the speed you can muster!"

Prince Gorsinski, embarked temporarily aboard the heavy cruiser *Berezina,* lowered his telescope and laughed loudly. "So the British are rowing themselves about the island! I wonder for what reason? I answer myself: John Frumm!" He paced the compass plat-form, hands behind his back, while the cruiser's captain and officer of the watch waited for their admiral's orders. They came soon. "A cutter, Captain, to be lowered and sent inshore with an armed party. Where is the gap in the coral reef—not the main entry where the British go in and out? The other."

"A little astern of us, Your Highness. We have passed it."

"Then take your ship back towards it, Captain."

The orders were passed and the *Berezina* came round to star-board. Before the cutter was sent away, the armed party was mustered for embarkation at the davits: a lieutenant was in charge, and was given his orders by Gorsinski in person: he was made responsible for the interception of the British whaler and its crew, and if men were landed from it, they were to be pursued and John Frumm was to be found and brought back to the *Berezina.*

"Failure," Gorsinski said, "will not be tolerated."

"I understand, Your Highness." Stiffly the officer saluted and left the compass platform. As the cruiser came abreast of the gap in the reef, the cutter, already lowered on the falls, was slipped to smack down on the flat Pacific calm.

Chapter 9

"SOMEONE in the trees, sir." The gunner's mate pointed. "I see the glint o' the moon, sir, on metal. It'll be a rifle or such or I'm a po bosun."

Halfhyde looked but saw nothing. "You're sure, Petty Officer Luke?"

"Dead sure, sir."

Halfhyde muttered an oath; they would have been seen now, that was certain. By this time the whaler was not far off the south-eastern side of the bay and its destination would be only too obvious, but there was nothing for it now but to continue. Halfhyde had expected hazards but the cutting out of John Frumm had been immensely complicated by the movement of the Russian cruiser. If Gorsinski's men entered the lagoon, Halfhyde knew it would be suicide to attempt to go back by water; the land route would have to be used, and then in all probability they would run into more native rifles than just the one spotted by the gunner's mate. If that happened, Captain Watkiss could become a casualty. An excitable officer at the best of times, he was little fitted to remain anonymous during a clandestine trek through the jungle. Loud tones of complaint and bombast would strike through to hostile ears and then even the faintest chance of success would be gone.

Halfhyde reached a sudden decision.

"Alter for the shore, Coxswain," he said. "Ninety degrees to port of your course."

"Aye, aye, sir." The boat came round; the shore was close, its deep sand gleaming silver. They could come under fire but that had to be risked: it was vital to stop the escape of the anonymous watcher in order to preserve such secrecy as was left. Halfhyde passed orders to the gunner's mate: the moment the landing-party had disembarked they were to move up the beach at the double, well spread out, and start combing the jungle fringe.

"We shall strike first," Halfhyde said, "then go for the cave. We have it in sight now. They'll not move John Frumm without our seeing."

The gunner's mate nodded and spat on his palms, rubbing them together as if preparing for a hand-to-hand fight. Within the minute the whaler took the sand, grounding softly, and the seamen jumped out with their rifles already loaded and the fixed bayonets gleaming bright. There was no delay: boots-and-gaiters pounded the sand, sinking in and making the run a hard slog. Ahead of them was silence. No counter-attack came. They reached the trees, and Halfhyde called a brief halt.

"Listen out," he said.

They listened, largely to their own heavy breathing. But after a moment Halfhyde's ears caught a sound a little way to his right: the creak and crackle of undergrowth as someone made a getaway. At once he passed the word; the armed men moved to the right, plunging into the jungle fringe, making no attempt at quietness: speed was what was needed now. As Halfhyde pushed ahead the sounds came back loudly. There was, he believed, a degree of panic; and some five minutes later he heard a heavy crash and a shout of pain. His revolver ready, he went ahead fast, scarcely feeling the lashing fronds across his face. He was still on the fringe and there was light penetrating from the moon; after a few more yards he saw the man ahead, lying gripped between two close-growing trees with a leg grotesquely twisted beneath his body. Halfhyde went forward with the gunner's mate. The man was an islander. Halfhyde reached down and removed the rifle from his grasp, passing it to the gunner's mate who slung it from his shoulder. Two seamen were called forward to lift the native. When his foot touched the ground he winced but seemed able to stand. It was nothing worse than a sprain. Halfhyde said, "Now you'll come with us."

Once again, Captain Watkiss had been moved out; this time, not far. After some hours alone in the darkness of the subterranean armoury, Dancey and Mulligan had rolled the stone aside and descended the ladder. Things, they said, were getting dangerous and John Frumm's influence was needed to stiffen the natives, who were tending to become overawed by the presence of so many ships and seamen. John Frumm was to reassure them, and would do so after dark that night.

"I fail to see the point," he said frigidly.

"Why?"

Watkiss said, "It's futile, is it not? You won't get away with your blasted schemes now. You can't possibly, with Her Majesty's ships lying off the island!"

"That's our worry," Dancey said. He seemed rattled, Watkiss thought; there was an unspoken suggestion of a last attempt. What fools some people were, to think for a moment that they could outwit the Fleet! However, fools or not, Dancey and Mulligan were quite set upon making use of him; it was sheer obstinacy, of course, but it had to be faced as fact. Watkiss listened to his instructions, which were simple enough: after dark there was to be a gathering of the islanders at which he was to be present, a revered father-figure whose word, or rather whose nod since he hadn't enough of the native lingo, was law. Dancey, who had picked up the islanders' tongue fairly easily, would do the talking and each time Dancey said the words "John Frumm," John Frumm was to nod his head.

"And don't bloody muck it up," Dancey said.

Captain Watkiss breathed hard down his nose; the man was a boor and there was nothing to be gained by responding to his rudeness, and there was probably nothing to be gained, either, by deliberately "mucking it up." Watkiss failed to see how he could, in any case; linguistically he would be unable to put his point of view to the natives—or rather, he could have done if given time, but Dancey and Mulligan would see that he wasn't, naturally. He could refuse to nod, perhaps; the blasted bandits could scarcely ill-treat John Frumm with the islanders looking on. But Dancey, who always seemed to cover everything, had also thought of that.

"Any funny business, any non-co-operation, and you get dealt with afterwards, see?" Dancey's tone was dangerous, vicious; it said all that was needed. The dealing would be cruel. Watkiss steeled himself; he was no coward. Dancey added, "Got that, mate?"

Watkiss saw red. He snapped, "Kindly don't address me as mate. I am a post captain of the Royal Navy, and—"

There was a laugh. "No, you're not, you're bloody John Frumm."

It was no use; Watkiss simmered in his handcuffs, feeling apoplexy to be close. There was some time to wait until it was dark enough for the Irishmen's purpose but at last Watkiss was lifted to his feet; the handcuffs were removed, both sets of them, and the revolver was pushed into his spine again.

Dancey said, "Up the ladder after Mulligan."

Mulligan climbed; Captain Watkiss followed as ordered. He emerged into moonlight, bright and clear. Distantly he saw the steaming lights of ships but he couldn't make out if they were British or Russian. Steaming lights . . . they hadn't anchored but of course there would be too great a depth of water. If they were British, then they were a pleasant sight, giving comfort. Her Majesty's arm was a long one. Captain Watkiss glowered as the revolver thrust powerfully into his back and, like a bullock given the goad, he was urged ahead through jungle country towards some rising ground that stood bare of trees like a bald patch on an otherwise hirsute head.

"Empty," Halfhyde said, having entered the cave. His voice was savage. He saw an element of the needle in the haystack; the island was not immensely large but the jungle provided a fine hiding place. He rounded on the native.

"John Frumm," he said.

No answer.

Halfhyde took a grip of the man's shoulders and shook him, hard. "John Frumm," he said again. "Where is he?" There was still no answer, but the flicker in the eyes told Halfhyde that the gist had been understood well enough. He glanced at the gunner's mate. "A little persuasion, Petty Officer Luke."

"Aye, aye, sir."

"The bayonets, all of them. Like the music hall act . . . the woman in the box, and the swords. Only there will be no box. You follow?"

There was a flash of teeth in the moonlight. "Aye, sir, that I do." The gunner's mate passed the orders and the seamen clustered round the now terrified native. They laid the points of the bayonets against the flesh. There was a high scream.

Halfhyde said, "No penetration, Petty Officer Luke. I doubt if it'll be necessary."

"Aye, aye, sir."

Halfhyde spoke to the native again. Once more he said, "John Frumm." For a moment there was no answer. Halfhyde met the eye of the gunner's mate. "A touch more pressure," he said. There was another scream and tears rolled down the man's face.

He said, "John Frumm, yes, I show."

Halfhyde blew out a long breath of relief. He said, "We shall lose no time now. Close escort, Petty Officer Luke. And a watch to the rear of us as well, against Prince Gorsinski!"

"Aye, aye, sir."

They moved away from the cave, behind the native guide, penetrating back into the jungle fringe, then deeper into the interior where the going was atrocious and they were forced down to a snail's pace for some distance. Halfhyde suffered a bounding impatience, wondering about the Russian movements; by this time a boat would very likely have entered the lagoon, and the cave, which was obvious enough, could soon be found and a spoor picked up. Every now and again he called a halt so that he could listen for a few moments. Though he heard nothing, his fears remained. They were leaving an excellent track behind them and if it took time to cut out Captain Watkiss, the Russians could catch up with them.

On they went, flailed at, their uniforms becoming torn, arms tiring with the constant necessity to shift branches from their path, legs growing heavier as they climbed over lying obstacles and dropped down the other side. After what had begun to seem an endless ordeal, they came into easier conditions. They were back once again in the fringe and the sea was in view. A little later the guide led them into the open for a short distance before plunging back into another neck of jungle that climbed an incline, gentle at first and then becoming steeper. They began to hear sounds from ahead: a ranting voice, hoarse and loud, speaking apparently in the island tongue, and every now and again the keening that had been heard outside the Residency.

They came clear of the trees, out into an open space, a circular space brightly lit by the moon which threw a curious greenish patina over an astonishing scene.

Halfhyde stared, feeling a prickle of apprehension run along his spine like ice-cold water. There was a vast crowd of men and women, loin-clothed, grass-skirted, swaying from the hips to their own intermittent keening, and the whole arena was surrounded with what looked like totem poles, curiously carved into evil-looking faces with madly staring wooden eyeballs like great marbles. Each totem pole was surmounted by the roughly carved replica of a boat with a mast and sail. It was something primeval, something out of a far-off past of strange gods and propitiations, something to chill the very blood with its suggestion of an unknown horror to be enacted, something evidently even more compelling to the native mind than the sight of the burning Residency. There was a smell of blood on the air, the result no doubt of sacrificial acts, of animal or even human throats slit to the honour and glory of weird gods. The boats on the totem poles . . . the cargo-cult, its believers in full session. The boats that would bring the cargoes . . . and the dreadful images on the totem poles were those of John Frumm. But this was no purely religious enaction; the speaker, the one whose ranting voice had been heard as they climbed, was a white man, bearded, tough-looking, clad in a once-white shirt and tattered trousers like a beachcomber. Another white man stood a few yards to the speaker's right: without a doubt these were Dancey and Mulligan. Just in front of the second man a squat figure was seated on a tree-stump; this squat person, who at intervals nodded his head and by so doing appeared to set off the dreadful keening, was Captain Watkiss.

Unseen as yet, Halfhyde moved forward with his revolver in his hand. He gestured the gunner's mate and the landing-party to close in behind him. Into the gunner's mate's ear he whispered, "As soon as I make our presence known, spread the men out—deploy right and left of me." He moved on, walking slowly, even now unseen by the intent people inside the ring of totem poles, unseen by John Frumm, nodding like a dummy on his tree-stump.

Then Halfhyde halted. He called out savagely, "You can stop your speechifying, Dancey or Mulligan, whichever you are. I have you covered and surrounded and if anyone makes a move towards me or my seamen, I shall open enfilading fire." He raised his revolver, pointing it directly at the speaker, who was standing on a crate labelled Dewar's Whisky.

There was a dead silence and no movement. No movement until, from the corner of an eye, Halfhyde saw the other white man, the one near Watkiss, reach for a rifle propped against a totem pole. Without hesitation he fired; the man went down with a crash and lay still. The moonlight showed blood welling from the chest. Halfhyde called to the gunner's mate to move his party in and take the man who had been speaking. He went forward himself, glancing at Watkiss: John Frumm seemed frozen to the tree-stump. Then he spoke.

"It's you, is it, Mr Halfhyde?"

"It is indeed, sir."

"Time you came." The voice was pettish. "What the devil is Commodore Bassinghorn doing I'd like to know!"

"Sleeping in his bunk, I shouldn't wonder, sir," Halfhyde answered tartly. He turned his back on Captain Watkiss, who was still in his brass hat and goatskin. Four seamen had gone in to arrest Dancey; one of them had dropped to the Irishman's rifle fire, and then Dancey had turned and run, pursued by the men of the landing-party towards the tree-line: death from the rifles caught him at the fringe. The natives were scattering now, running in panic down the slopes into the jungle, to the fury of Captain Watkiss who called out to Halfhyde.

"Mr Halfhyde, the natives. Have them stopped!"

"They've nothing to answer for in my opinion, sir. They've been the dupes, the cat's-paws for Dancey and Mulligan."

"That's got nothing to do with it!"

"I disagree, sir. They'll return to their sanity now that you've been punctured and the arrival of the cargoes put forward another thousand years or so. In any case, I have far too few men to stem the rush."

Captain Watkiss was looking greenly furious beneath the moon. "I shall have you court martialled for damned impertinence and disobedience of orders! I shall have you drummed out of the Queen's service! This whole thing's a blasted disgrace—I should never have been abandoned; it's a reproach to the Fleet." He paused, breathing hard. "Mr Halfhyde, are you or are you not paying me the courtesy of listening to me?"

Halfhyde, who had been in an attitude of listening to other sounds, said, "Your pardon, sir. I must ask you to keep silent while I listen for my duty."

"Duty, what duty? I'm—"

"The Russians, sir."

"What Russians?"

Halfhyde hissed, "Prince Gorsinski's Russians, sir. Gorsinski is after you and I fancy he is not far off." He moved away towards the gunner's mate, calling for men to take position around Captain Watkiss, a valuable property. Watkiss got up from his tree-stump and looked this way and that, seeking Russians and appearing immensely agitated. Hearing a rattle of equipment from the jungle trees, Halfhyde swung round. On the perimeter of the arena he saw shadowy figures, moving inwards behind rifles with bayonets fixed.

Chapter 10

"WHAT IS IT, Mr Halfhyde, what is it?" Captain Watkiss was much on edge, his monocle jiggling about on the end of its silk toggle and looking incongruous against the dirty goatskin.

One of the guarding seamen answered. "It's the Russkies, sir."

"What?"

"They've got 'ere, sir—"

"Damned impertinence! They have no right to set foot on British territory." Captain Watkiss raised his voice. "Mr Halfhyde, you are to see to it that the blasted Russians leave immediately, they're nothing but damned dagoes and that's fact—I said it."

Facing the advance of a Russian officer, Halfhyde heard Watkiss's petulant tones and grinned briefly: Captain Watkiss was right back to his old form now; having shed the mantle of John Frumm he had quickly resumed the status of post captain and never mind the half-pay list. In the meantime, trouble was approaching. Russians were moving in from all sides, a strong force of them, such that indicated the landing of more than a single boat-load. Their bayonetted rifles were aimed to cover the whole British party. Matters were on a knife-edge in Halfhyde's view; the Russians could well risk opening fire and thus the creation of an international incident. Prince Gorsinski was not the man to shrink from a fraught situation and was well known to be harsh even to the death in enforcing his orders to his officers and men. As the Russian lieutenant approached with his revolver drawn, clear beneath the moon, Halfhyde met his eye calmly.

He said, "I think you presume, Lieutenant."

"In what way?" The English was good.

"By landing on British sovereign territory—by landing without permission from His Excellency the Governor, and by landing under arms."

"I have my admiral's orders," the Russian said stiffly. "They will be obeyed."

"At risk of your men standing into danger. If there is fire, it will be returned, have no doubt about that, my friend!"

The Russian officer gave a shrug of contempt. "You and your men are surrounded and covered. I have the advantage. It will be your seamen who will die. But fighting is not necessary. What I ask on my admiral's behalf is simple enough." He paused. "The person in the goatskin, whom I think is John Frumm—"

"Do you indeed?"

"Yes. He is required by my admiral, aboard the flagship." The lieutenant turned away from Halfhyde and stalked towards his quarry, who was standing like a belligerent rum-tub behind the stalwart seamen of his personal guard. "You are the man said to be John Frumm, I think?"

"No!" Watkiss snapped. "I am a post captain of the British Fleet! Can't you see my blasted cap, or are you blind?"

"A British captain?" The Russian seemed disconcerted. "The cap is yours?"

"Yes!" Watkiss hauled in his monocle and placed it in his eye-socket. The moon struck brilliance from its gold rim. "I am Captain Watkiss of Her Majesty's Navy and I demand—"

"What ship, sir, may I enquire?"

"No ship at present," Captain Watkiss answered with reluctance. "I am here unofficially . . . to observe." He saw no point in attempting to explain half-pay to a dago and found no need to go into the matter of his shipwreck. To question him at all was cheek. "If you will be good enough to take your blasted men away from Her Majesty's property, I shall be put aboard the British squadron by the good offices of Mr—"

"Have a care, sir," Halfhyde called out sharply. He had no wish to be named in the Russian's presence. "The less said, the better!"

"Oh, balls and bang-me-arse, Mr Halfhyde, how can one possibly remain silent in the circumstances? Kindly get rid of these people and have me taken aboard the *Port Royal* at once."

"I—"

"Oh, don't argue, Mr Halfhyde, you know very well I detest argument, *detest* it." Watkiss turned pompously back to the Russian lieutenant. "If you refuse to co-operate, my dear sir, a strong protest will go from my government to yours and after that I wouldn't care to be in your shoes, damned if I would. Now, then!" He stared angrily from behind the seamen, who were virtually obscuring him altogether.

The Russian pulled at his chin. "You are John Frumm. This I still believe."

"Oh dear, oh dear!" Watkiss fumed, moving up and down on the balls of his feet. "*I am not John Frumm!* The stupid natives *thought* I was! That's all, don't you see? It was all a mistake. It can be very easily explained."

"Aha. Then, sir, perhaps you would be good enough to explain it to my admiral in person?"

"I don't see why I should, and I shall do no such thing," Captain Watkiss answered promptly. "It's got nothing to do with your blasted admiral, whatsisname."

"Admiral Prince Gorsinski, sir. Kinsman to His Imperial Majesty the Czar of all the Russias—"

"Yes, we've met before," Watkiss said distantly.

"Who insists upon your presence—that is to say, the presence of John Frumm. As a British officer, sir—mistaken for John Frumm—you would not wish to expose your seamen to bloodshed. Of this I am certain."

"Yes, true." Watkiss nodded vigorously. "But if you were so foolish as to open fire, your Czar would have your head, Mr Whoever-you-are. Queen Victoria would despatch a battle fleet to bombard your blasted ports—your Czar wouldn't be pleased with *that*—"

"A risk we both take, sir," the Russian interrupted, smiling. "Queen Victoria might not be pleased that by refusing a polite request from Prince Gorsinski, you had brought about a difficult situation leading, perhaps, to war."

"H'm."

Some advantage was showing through, and the Russian pressed upon it, waving his arms—like a nancy-boy in Watkiss's opinion. "It is so simple! A personal meeting, that is all, to satisfy my admiral. Then you will be at once given a boat to board the British flagship. My admiral will naturally behave properly."

"Well . . . one has to concede he's a gentleman, of course. Mr Halfhyde?"

"Sir?"

"What do you think?"

"I think it would be insanity, sir—"

"I call that impertinent, Mr Halfhyde, and typical of you."

"Nevertheless, sir, I say it again and with renewed emphasis." Halfhyde's voice was harsh. "If you spare one moment to give it proper thought—"

"Oh, damn you—"

"Which I think you have not so far done, sir, then you would see that even to be *believed* by the natives to be John Frumm is enough for—"

"Hold your tongue, Mr Halfhyde, or I shall have you before a Court Martial the moment I reach a suitable port."

"I—"

"*Keep silent!*" Captain Watkiss, still without his telescope, waved the thigh bone as though about to burst through his guard and attack Halfhyde with it. "I am no lily-livered coward who fails to put his men's welfare before his own. I thank God for making me a man, not a mouse. I intend to go aboard the Russian flagship and establish my *bona fides* before joining the squadron, and that's that." He glared at Halfhyde. "You have the curious ability to give all the wrong answers, have you not? Any senior officer would be well advised to act on a course diametrically opposed to your views and advice—which I suppose does give you a certain opposite value!"

Halfhyde was left in a quandary. Prepared as he was, in fact, to disregard Watkiss's orders and make the attempt to cut the *ci-devant* John Frumm out from under the Russians' noses, he recognized fully the dangers of so doing: he would lose many men without a doubt if the rifles opened—he was greatly outnumbered. Besides, Captain Watkiss might possibly have a point. Prince Gorsinski would certainly not be expecting John Frumm to be a senior British naval officer and he might have the wind taken from his sails by the appearance of Captain Watkiss who would undoubtedly be vocal in his own interests. If that proved to be the case, and if Watkiss was subsequently restored to the British Fleet, then any sacrifice of lives would have been wasted, and cruelly wasted at that. Halfhyde's concern for his seamen won the day, and he watched in chagrin as Watkiss went off in his goatskin with the Russian landing-party. He had an unkind and insubordinate hope that the Russians might keep him after all. They would be more than welcome to him and would have had enough of his tantrums by the time they reached Vladivostok again.

Halfhyde sighed and turned to his gunner's mate. "All right, Petty Officer Luke, that ends our duty—for now!"

Luke nodded, and ran a finger along the blade of his cutlass, looking regretful that it hadn't been used. "Back to the ship, sir?"

"Yes. As fast as possible. A report must go to the commodore, urgently."

The gunner's mate mustered the seamen and formed them up for the trek back through the jungle. It was a difficult journey and before they had found the track they had become lost on more than one occasion. The result was much delay. As they left the jungle fringe at long last and marched in for the jetty and the *Talisman,* the sky had lightened with the dawn; the day looked cheerful and the bright sun helped in some measure to dispel the gloom of the night and its weird happenings. But that sun failed to reveal the Russian ships: the waters off Zanatu stood empty but for the *Port Royal* and the *Plantagenet.*

Halfhyde swore roundly and pressed on fast for the *Talisman.* As he approached the brow, his first lieutenant emerged from the superstructure aft to salute him aboard.

Halfhyde returned the salute perfunctorily. "Good morning, Mr Halliburton. I see that the Russian squadron has left the island."

"Yes, sir."

"At what time?"

"A little after two bells in the morning watch, sir."

"I see. Were signals exchanged with the commodore?"

Halliburton nodded. "Yes, sir. Just leave-taking signals, so far as they could be read from here."

Halfhyde gave a grunt; it was obvious enough that Gorsinski would not have reported the shanghai-ing of Captain Watkiss if that was what had happened. Halfhyde asked, "Did any boats go off from the Russians towards our ships?"

"None were reported, sir. If they'd been seen, they would have been reported to me."

"Yes. In that case, Mr Halliburton, you will call away a boat. I propose to board the *Port Royal* immediately."

Captain Watkiss, politely accorded the freedom of the Russian flagship's quarterdeck—as Prince Gorsinski had remarked, the South Pacific contained gaolers enough in the form of the ravening, sharp-toothed sharks—glowered back in the direction of Zanatu, now vanished astern. The Russians were diabolical, real fiends. Gorsinski had been adamant: Watkiss was not going to be handed back to the British. He was to continue as John Frumm, but not on Zanatu. Watkiss, walking the sun-drenched quarterdeck, reflected bitterly upon the sentence he had not allowed Halfhyde to finish: the native belief in his John Frumm identity had proved, undeniably, more than enough for Gorsinski. The word about John Frumm would have spread already to all the islands. He was going to be made to work hard in the Russian interest—or so that fellow Gorsinski thought.

Captain Watkiss ground his teeth savagely. Of course, he wouldn't help the Russians, that went without saying, but refusal was going to be very uncomfortable. Gorsinski was a man of vile temper and high-handed methods who was known to act first and think afterwards.

It was a nasty situation.

During the interview with Prince Gorsinski in the admiral's palatial quarters, Watkiss had made the point that Commodore Bassinghorn would make all speed to his rescue the moment the word reached him from Halfhyde. Gorsinski had dismissed this with a contemptuous wave of a be-ringed hand—diamonds and emeralds had glittered, to Watkiss's disgust, but all dagoes were nancy-boys, of course, admirals as much as lieutenants. Gorsinski had remarked that his ships had the legs of the British by very many knots and the Pacific was an immensely large area to cover. He was unworried; but spoke of Halfhyde, whose name had already been mentioned to him by the lieutenant in charge of the landing-party.

"This Halfhyde. The name of his ship, please?"

"I've no idea," Watkiss answered promptly. He was well aware of the enmity between Halfhyde and Gorsinski, an affair of long standing made much worse by Halfhyde's actions when under his, Watkiss's, own command in the Fourth Motor Torpedo-Boat Flotilla a few years earlier. He was suffering a twinge of conscience now for having so blatantly mentioned Halfhyde's name within hearing of the Russians.

"I do not think you tell the truth, Captain."

"Truth be buggered, my dear sir, I don't concern myself with the appointments of junior lieutenants."

Prince Gorsinski nodded suavely, though there was an angry glitter in his eyes as he paced his day-cabin, towering over the plump seated figure of Captain Watkiss . . . and that, Watkiss thought, was another thing: Gorsinski, like all tall people— Halfhyde himself included—acted as though there were virtue in his very height, feeling himself superior to short men. This was balls, of course, when everyone knew that short men, like Nelson, had far better minds and intellectual powers, but there it was. Tall men had an advantage in their own eyes, an unfair one. Gorsinski went on, "At least I know he must be aboard one of the ships. I would guess the torpedo-boat destroyer at the jetty. I am right, am I not?"

"I told you I don't know," Watkiss answered crossly. "What about *me,* may I ask?"

Gorsinski smiled. "I think I need not repeat what I have told you already, except to say that you will retain your goatskin and the monkey's skull and the thigh bone. They are part of your aura."

Watkiss, as now he paced the quarterdeck while the sun climbed the bright blue sky, pulled out his turnip-shaped watch and he studied it. He thought about the further words uttered by Prince Gorsinski: he was to be allowed two exercise periods each day and for the rest of the time was to be confined to a small cabin previously occupied by a junior Russian lieutenant where he was to sit in state with the skull and thigh bone and the goatskin . . . the flagship's seamen, Gorsinski had said, like so many Russians of the lower class, were as superstitious as were the natives of the South Pacific themselves; and if they could be led to a belief in the embodiment of John Frumm then so much the better when they went ashore in the islands to mingle with the trusting inhabitants. The gospel was always more effectively spread by the true believer.

Bassinghorn was a much worried man after Halfhyde had made his report. "You've no idea where Gorsinski might be heading?" he asked.

"None, sir. Except that it'll presumably be towards some of the islands where the Russians hope to extend their influence and set up trading posts. The charts and Sailing Directions might provide some clues, I would suggest."

Bassinghorn nodded. "Yes. I've already made a study of them

together with Sir Wilbraham. But taking into account that Gorsinski, like ourselves, will have a need to coal his ships, I believe he'll make north for the island of Paravela in the first instance."

"A Japanese possession, sir."

"True. But they offer a bunkering facility. It's as good a guess as any! In the meantime, I shall prepare for sea at once. You must return aboard your own ship, my dear Halfhyde. I shall leave the island within the next half hour, taking a northerly course."

"Yes, sir." Halfhyde got to his feet, then hesitated. "There will be a magnet, sir."

"A magnet?"

"Myself, sir. My name became uttered in the hearing of the Russian lieutenant—this was unfortunate, but inevitable—"

"Gorsinski will know by this time?"

"Undoubtedly, sir. And he'll want to get his hands on me. It's just possible I could weigh more upon his mind than John Frumm, who may not be immediately required—"

"And you're a case for immediacy?"

Halfhyde nodded. "I am, sir. He has Captain Watkiss, but he hasn't got me—yet! I've a feeling Prince Gorsinski may decide to lay a trail and when we're once again in company with his ships he'll find some subterfuge to have me delivered into his hands." He laughed, but without humour. "An exchange, per-haps, with Captain Watkiss!"

"One that I would most certainly never agree to, Halfhyde."

Halfhyde laughed again. "I'm grateful, sir, but we should remem-ber Prince Gorsinski has more powerful guns than we have."

Bassinghorn nodded, and pressed a bell-push on the bulk-head by the side of his roll-top desk. When a seaman runner entered from the lobby outside the commodore's quarters, Bassinghorn despatched him for the commander, the navigating officer, and the fleet engineer. Taking his leave, Halfhyde made his way to the quarterdeck, where he asked the officer of the watch to hail his boat, lying off the starboard accommodation-ladder. As he was pulled back across the placid water towards the island he heard the bugles sounding from the *Port Royal* and the *Plantagenet* and within moments saw the seamen doubling to their stations. Bassinghorn was losing no time.

As soon as he was aboard the *Talisman* Halfhyde ordered his first lieutenant to prepare for sea.

"I've already passed the orders, sir," Halliburton said.

Halfhyde smiled, and clapped him on the shoulder. "Good! I'm delighted you find no need to wait for orders when it's obvious what they're going to be." He went for'ard to his navigating bridge and joined Stallybrass, who was now taking a watch in place of the dead sub-lieutenant. The torpedo-gunner touched his cap-peak in an old-fashioned salute. Halfhyde said, "You may have your chance yet, Mr Stallybrass. Your torpedoes. Commodore Bassinghorn is in no mood to deal gently with Prince Gorsinski!"

"I'm glad to hear it, sir. Them Russkies, they're too big for their boots, sir."

"Too big indeed." Halfhyde looked out at the shore. A number of natives had clustered by the jungle fringe; they had an unhappy, uncertain look rather than one of war. Neither the Russian presence nor Mulligan and Dancey had been a benison; the peaceful world of Zanatu's inhabitants lay shattered with the burned-out shell of the Residency and the departure of the Governor and his staff. Now they were on their own, at least until the distant British Queen in Windsor Castle made her wishes known—and Victoria the Good might well be very angry at what had been inflicted by her subjects upon her personal representative and her island possession, and her response might be harsh. The natives stood subdued by fear; Halfhyde wished them well as his ship was reported ready to proceed. He passed the orders for bringing her stern first off the rickety jetty and then turned her to head for the entry channel through the reef. He kept his engine slow until he was safely outside, then increased to full and turned to overtake the *Port Royal* and the *Plantagenet,* already distant to the north with their ensigns blowing out along the wind made by their passage and their guns trained to the fore-and-aft line. They were a heartening sight and Halfhyde was glad enough to be free of the land and back upon the broad sea; but if action were joined in the days ahead, then no man in the squadron could fail to be aware that the bigger guns of Prince Gorsinski would make mincemeat of them as the great shells flung in thunder and flame through the unarmoured British sides to explode bloodily along the confined mess decks and the gundecks that served the sponsoned armament.

Chapter 11

PRINCE GORSINSKI paced the admiral's bridge aboard the *Catherine the Great,* frowning thoughtfully and looking down from time to time at the magnificent gun-turrets that carried his main armament. His mind was filled with thoughts of Lieutenant St Vincent Halfhyde of the Royal Navy; and those thoughts were in the extreme. It was bad enough to have been bested so many times by a mere lieutenant; the fact that the lieutenant was British and thus out of his jurisdiction made it so much the worse to bear. Gorsinski came from a long line of fighting men, some of them soldiers, some of them sailors like himself—admirals and generals all. And all of them filled with a fierce pride in their reputations and their lineage.

Gorsinski looked again at his guns, then astern at the guns of the *Berezina* and the *Smolensk.* He smiled, and rubbed his hands together. Revenge would be sweet, and could be very close at hand if luck and canniness went his way. It was certain enough that the British ships would give chase. Let them!

Gorsinski stopped his pacing. "Flag Captain," he said.

"Yes, Your Highness?"

"Reduce to half speed."

The flag captain stared. "Half speed, Your Highness?"

Gorsinski spoke frigidly. "I do not repeat my orders, Flag Captain."

"But Your Highness . . . the British will overtake—"

"Are you afraid of the British, Flag Captain—afraid of their pea-shooter guns?"

The flag captain drew himself up. "By no means, Your Highness. That is an unworthy suggestion. But I think it unwise to court an action."

"Do you, Flag Captain?"

"In my view," the flag captain persisted, "discretion is called for. We have the man John Frumm. Thus far, we have won, Your Highness. Would it not be better to remain as anonymous as possible now, rather than deliberately to run against a British squadron who will demand the return of John Frumm?"

"I think not. I have other demands upon the British commodore."

The flag captain pulled at his beard. "I would have a care, Your Highness. His Imperial Majesty will not wish an action."

"That is my concern, not yours," Gorsinski snapped. "I am allied to the blood, and I act always in the best interest of my Czar." He turned away from his flag captain and resumed his pacing as the order for reduced speed was passed to the flagship's engine-room and repeated by flag signal to the ships in company. Like his face, Gorsinski's stride was arrogant and self-assured; his lips, always thin, were set in a pencil line between the facial hair. He gave one more order: John Frumm was to be brought to him on his bridge. John Frumm, in his proper identity of Captain Watkiss, had been known to Prince Gorsinski in the past. Gorsinski regarded Captain Watkiss as a pompous fool, a prancing buffoon; but he had his uses.

Captain Watkiss drew the goatskin about his short body and glared up at Prince Gorsinski. "I shall not co-operate in any way at all. I—"

"You will be ill advised to refuse."

"Ill advised, my backside. I am a post captain in Her Majesty's Fleet! I shall not act against Her Majesty's interests whatever you have to say about it."

Gorsinski smiled. "I am related to my Czar."

Watkiss sniffed. "You may be related to whomsoever you wish, my dear sir, you fail to impress me. You're a Russian and I don't give a fish's tit for foreigners; they're not British. What does it matter to me that you're related to the blasted Czar, a fact I was already aware of in any case?"

"Have a care, Captain." Gorsinski's face had flushed at the slighting reference to the Czar. "What I mean to convey is this: whatever I decide to do will receive support. You are power-less—and my request is simple, is it not, and innocuous?"

"Simple perhaps. Scarcely innocuous." Captain Watkiss swiped angrily at a strand of goat's hair that had strayed towards his mouth. "You wish me to shout across at the *Port Royal* when she overtakes, asking for Mr Halfhyde to be put aboard you on some ridiculous excuse. I don't call that innocuous to Halfhyde, damned if I do!"

"But to yourself innocuous, is this not so?"

"I happen to know where my duty lies, thank you. Do your worst to me—if you dare." Watkiss waved his arms about. "I shall never put my junior officers in peril and that's fact—I said it."

"I see." Gorsinski's tone was ominous. "In that case, you put every man of Commodore Bassinghorn's squadron in the most mortal danger. It is one man against many—against many hundreds."

"Ha!" Captain Watkiss drew in the toggle of his monocle and put the shining glass in place. "Are you telling me that you'll start an action, Prince?"

Gorsinski said, "I shall not merely start an action, Captain. I shall finish it. I shall send all three ships to the bottom of the Pacific, and shall not pick up survivors."

"I call that dastardly. You'll be court martialled."

Gorsinski laughed. "Survivors can tell stories. So can I. I shall note it in my log that the British opened upon me and I had no option but to use my guns. And I shall have caught them, as you British would say, with their trousers about their ankles!"

Watkiss gaped. He was almost speechless, but managed to say, "Such lies. I considered you to be a gentleman. I now see that you're nothing but a knave, Prince or not."

"A knave in your eyes, perhaps. But now you have the option —it is your choice. Either you call across for Lieutenant Halfhyde to be sent aboard my flagship to offer proof to me of who you are, so that you can be sent back—or you witness the destruction of the British squadron. Your answer?"

Watkiss spluttered. "It's a stupid idea in any case. Halfhyde could identify me through his telescope—any fool would know that! There would be no need to send him across."

"Your answer?" Gorsinski was implacable. The British would know something else too: their Captain Watkiss would be at risk if Halfhyde was not delivered. In any navy, a post captain must be considered before a junior lieutenant.

"My answer," Watkiss replied with dignity but with an odd sensation forming in his stomach, "is no."

"Think again," Gorsinski said. "Think again about the ships and your British seamen, of the shattered bodies in the water, of the steam-scalded and burned stokers in the boiler-rooms, of the terrible sight when a great ship plunges to the depths to be flattened like a box of cardboard in the tremendous pressures at the bottom of the Pacific Ocean." The Russian's face was alight with strange fires of its own, almost a possessed face, but Watkiss thought, fiddlesticks, the fellow's laying it on too thick. There was, he convinced himself, bluff in the air.

The day was moving towards sunset when Halfhyde's yeoman of signals reported: "Message coming through from the commodore, sir." He read off the semaphore arms waving from Bassinghorn's flag deck. "Russian ships in sight ten miles dead ahead, sir."

Halfhyde turned to his first lieutenant. "Mr Halliburton, pipe first degree of readiness."

"Aye, aye, sir." Halliburton passed the order to the boatswain's mate and as the pipe sounded round the ship the guns' crews and torpedomen moved to their stations. Halliburton asked, "Do you expect action right away, sir?"

Halfhyde shook .his head. "You'll notice I've not sounded action stations, Mr Halliburton, and you'll appreciate the essential difference! No—I mean to be ready, that's all, in advance of orders from the commodore. I expect them at any moment." He was right; within the next minute there was more signalling from the *Port Royal*. All ships of the squadron were to go to first degree of readiness but the guns' crews were merely to remain handy for their guns, keeping in cover so as not to appear to offer a warlike aspect to the Russians. If the commodore's bugles sounded, this would indicate an emergency and the guns would be manned immediately and brought to bear on the Russian squadron. As the *Talisman* steamed ahead, Halfhyde brought up his telescope and searched the seas. Though visible, apparently, from the high masthead of the *Port Royal*, the Russians were not yet within sight from the small torpedo-boat destroyer. Soon, however, the masts and fighting-tops were seen; and then the ships themselves, coloured by a splendid sunset as a blood-red orb sank to touch the western horizon.

Halfhyde looked at them with foreboding: proximity to Prince Gorsinski was something he had always hoped to avoid. He had no doubts at all that should the Russian aristocrat get his hands upon his old adversary the future would hold only death or Siberia. The one hope appeared to be Bassinghorn's determination to hold on to him. An unknown quantity was Watkiss himself, who might possibly find some lever with which to force Gorsinski's hand; but this was the forlornest of hopes. Captain Watkiss was not a man of swift and penetrating mind. Normally his mental processes revolved around mundane matters concerned with the importance of not being argued with, the punishment of persons who dared to use the many ladders aboard his command—when he had one—marked "Captain Only," the physical cleanliness of midshipmen, and the preservation of his cheese supply against the depradations of hot climates. Matters of tactics, of strategy, and stratagems, did not come easily to his comprehension and the consideration of such usually led to a violent outburst of temper.

The two squadrons closed. Halfhyde was certain of one thing: he had been proved right in his suggestion to Bassinghorn that Prince Gorsinski might angle for a meeting at sea. Even now, he could easily have drawn away from the British ships if he had wished but he was showing no sign of doing so.

Meanwhile, Bassinghorn was making signals, and making them with the all-round lamp at his foremasthead so that they could be read from the ships of his own squadron as well as by Prince Gorsinski's signalman. Aboard the *Talisman,* the yeoman made his report.

"From Commodore Long Range Squadron, sir, to Admiral

Prince Gorsinski. *I have reason to believe you have a British naval captain embarked under duress. I await your explanation and the return forthwith of Captain Watkiss.*"

Halfhyde caught Halliburton's eye. "The commodore's making no bones, Mr Halliburton. It's touch and go now."

The first lieutenant nodded. The sun was moving further down now, flattening as it sank below the hard line of the horizon. The sky was a sheer brilliance of colour but very soon now the daylight would be gone. On *Talisman's* bridge they waited in growing tension, the guns' crews ready for action orders. Below on the upper deck Mr Stallybrass stroked his torpedo-tubes with a proprietorial, even a loving, hand. His tin fish were good and would run true, slamming into the Russians' side plating to explode and shatter and cause screaming havoc. With luck, they might penetrate the armoured belt covering the magazines and then there would be an almighty holocaust.

"Russian answering, sir!"

Halfhyde read off the winking light from the *Catherine the Great* before the yeoman reported. "*I have no British officer. I have John Frumm. I do not understand your request.*"

Halfhyde said, "If that's the line he's going to take, the commodore's in something of a cleft stick. Captain Watkiss was undeniably John Frumm when found!"

"What do you think will happen now, sir?" Halliburton asked in some anxiety.

"It's in the lap of the gods, Mr Halliburton. Two determined officers are facing each other, and such a confrontation often leads to war."

The daylight was fading fast now; the waters darkened and the opposing squadrons lay as black shadows illuminated on their proper arcs by their steaming lights, red and green and white. There was a hint of a wind now, coming up from the south-east. For the time being at any rate there was no more signalling: it was as though each side was waiting for the other. Halfhyde hoped that Gorsinski, when faced with the actual decision to make an issue of it, might find some touch of prudence holding him back. The motive of personal revenge, though strong, might at the last moment not appear strong enough to be sustained after a clash of arms with all its consequences.

The minutes ticked away.

Captain Watkiss had been feeling the sharp horns of an agonizing dilemma, all day. Gorsinski's flamboyant speech was making him uneasy now that he had had time to reflect upon the awful spectacle envisaged by the admiral. It might not, after all, be bluff. There was that reputation of Gorsinski's: the man who acted first and thought afterwards. And Halfhyde?

Halfhyde was Halfhyde and a blasted nuisance mostly, a thorn in his side throughout far too many past commissions on Her Majesty's service. Was his safety worth the possible sacrifice of hundreds of good British tars?

Frankly, it was not; and no one could lay blame at his, Watkiss's, door for taking the broader view. The Admiralty could never fault him. And of course Halfhyde really wouldn't be allowed to suffer at Gorsinski's hands. The British people would never stand for that! The very strongest representations would go from the Foreign Office, that noble bastion of British pride— so long as one could ignore the fact that it was staffed by the most dreadful collection of clerkly pimps. Watkiss's duty was plain: bluff could not be banked upon and it was up to him to keep the British Fleet in being.

He went to the admiral's bridge. "I shall do as you ask, Admiral," he said.

"Ah." Courteously enough Gorsinski turned; there was a smile on his face, but it was an unpleasant one. "And what was that, pray?"

"Why, to show myself and ask for Mr Halfhyde to be sent across to identify me. Then I can be released."

Gorsinski said, "It is now too dark."

"Oh, nonsense, a light can be put upon me, can it not?"

"Possibly. The concept is now redundant," Gorsinski said. "I have said you are John Frumm." He paused, then added, "I have changed my mind about Lieutenant Halfhyde."

"Oh." Captain Watkiss appeared disconcerted. "You don't want him after all, then? What about me?"

"I want him alive," Gorsinski said calmly. "If I were to open fire—"

"Good God, I would have imagined you'd have thought of that earlier, my dear sir!"

The Russian shrugged. There was a smile on his lips still, and it was still unpleasant. "Great commanders . . . have you never found the need to change your mind, Captain?"

"Upon occasions, yes."

"There you are, then! In daylight there would have been a chance. It would have been worth the risk. In the hours of darkness—no. I had expected to be overtaken before this, you understand, and I would have concentrated my fire on the cruisers whilst sending a boarding party to the torpedo-boat destroyer, where I believe Lieutenant Halfhyde would have been found in command. He has held a similar appointment before, as both you and I know very well."

"Yes, yes, yes. But your idea was for him to be *sent across.*"

"True. But I came to believe that the British commodore would not sanction this and so there would have been action. For reasons already given, Captain, I do not propose to enter into night action."

Gorsinski turned away and strode across his bridge. Watkiss kept silent, but simmered angrily inside at the way in which Halfhyde seemed continually to land him in impossible predicaments even when, as now, the two of them were far from serving in the same ship or flotilla. If only the fool had taken him aboard Bassinghorn's ship when he'd been all ready to go . . . but it was no use wishing, the die was cast and here he was. He rose and fell on the balls of his feet, trying desperately to see his way clear through this particular predicament; he had no intention of ending his days as John Frumm in the service of the blasted Russians but it began to look very much as though he was going to have to unless Bassinghorn took some positive steps to aid him. Even those steps, if positive enough, could be dangerous: Captain Watkiss's heart sank. He would be smack on the receiving end of any British gunfire.

He drew his goatskin cloak tightly around his body. The night had grown suddenly cold.

Chapter 12

"THERE'S A TYPHOON coming up," Halfhyde said. He had felt the wind and noted the drop in temperature. The night was blackening fast from the south-east quarter; the moon and stars were not going to show that night. The barometer was plummeting. He had scarcely spoken when the masthead light began winking aboard the *Port Royal*. Bassinghorn was ordering his squadron to batten down to fight the storm and to scatter to a safe and manoeuvrable distance. The rendezvous when they had all come through would be the coaling station on the island of Paravela to which they had been bound from Zanatu.

"And what about Gorsinski?" Halfhyde asked rhetorically. He laid his telescope upon the *Catherine the Great,* now turning away. Bugles sounded, ordering precautions similar to those put in hand by the British. Halfhyde let out a long breath. He had been given a respite, but for how long? It was a pound to a penny Gorsinski also would be heading ultimately for Paravela in order to bunker his squadron, as Bassinghorn had prophesied originally. But that must wait; for now, his ship was his first concern. Until the typhoon had passed, he would not leave his navigating bridge.

The ships, soon widespread across the terrible turbulence of the sea, heaved and fell, climbing mountainous waves and swooping down into the valleys. Their plates protested at the immensity of the strain. Solid water dropped aboard, cascading along the decks, smashing boats and davits, battering thunderously at the stowed anchors and drumming the great cables on the steel chafe-plates beneath them, a din that echoed through the fo'c'sles, joining the awesome racket from the navel-pipes and cable-lockers as the heavy links lurched about and clanged vociferously against the bulkheads. On the navigating bridges the British and Russian officers clung for support to handy stanchions, dashing seawater from their eyes and feeling the soak of it beneath their oilskins and sou'westers. They were drenched to a man and would remain so until the weather moderated. There was no heat now: all galley fires had been drawn in the interest of safety, for fire at sea was something feared by all mariners. Only in the busy, red-lit stokeholds was there warmth, and there the atmosphere was almost untenable as the stokers lurched with filled shovels across the steel deck-plating to hurl their loads into the gaping mouths of the furnaces. It was a murderous task. The decks seemed alive as they heaved and fell, and scattering red-hot coal brought screams and oaths from the luckless black gang. Aboard the Russian ships, the stoker petty officers had been issued with revolvers. If any man should show a lack of attention to his duty, he would be shot out of hand as a warning to the others. No ship could risk any reduction in steam pressure.

Captain Watkiss was in extremis, passing a wretched night.

When the typhoon had struck he had been ordered off the admiral's bridge and back to his borrowed cabin, a small place and not very clean. The Russians were not clean people . . . very different from British seamen, but that stood to reason and had to be put up with.

Captain Watkiss took off the goatskin and laid it at the foot of his bunk. He placed his uniform cap tenderly upon a hook; apart from his long white shorts that cap was his last remaining link with the British Fleet, a symbol of what in fact he still was. Opening a drawer—opening several in the hope of finding one empty—he thrust the detested monkey's skull and the thigh bone on top of a pile of Russian vests. Then he lay down on the bunk, feeling a queasiness in his stomach, due not to incipient seasickness but to a terrible fear.

Watkiss had never suffered a typhoon before despite having served—with the wretched Halfhyde as it happened—on the China station. He had been lucky; now his luck had run out. And it had to run out aboard a blasted Russian ship! The Russians were poor seamen as compared with the British—that stood to reason too.

He would probably be lost at sea.

Captain Watkiss, who had hitherto regarded ships' chaplains in much the same way as he regarded foreigners, wished for the presence of one now to lead him in prayer to the Almighty. God would show mercy if approached properly. Beseeched, he would calm the raging of the seas so that even a Russian could cope with them. But there was no chaplain available and the seas raged on alarmingly. The noise was quite appalling . . . the *Catherine the Great* seemed to be breaking apart and the cabin was almost turning somersaults. Watkiss lay stretched out like a violin string, jamming feet and hands to whatever was available so that he would not be cast from the bunk. The din grew worse; a tremendous bang came upon the deckhead above him as something toppled down and smote the main deck. Anxiously Watkiss peered up, seeking leaks. His fear mounted: there *was* a leak—the deck had been sprung and water, cold and salt, began to descend on the bunk. Not a lot so far, but leaks always tended to widen under the impact of stress. Soon after this a colossal sea smashed with a giant's hand against his port, and more water appeared, oozing round the clamped-down deadlight that obscured the heavy glass.

Goodness gracious!

Watkiss clambered out of the bunk, shaking in every limb.
He took care to retain a tight hold of the screwed-down wash-
hand basin while he sank upon his knees beside the bunk and
placed his free hand before his face in humble prayer and sup-
plication. Just one hand . . . God would surely understand that
he was a seaman and seamen always, by long tradition, kept one
hand for themselves the other for the ship. Although unused to
prayer, his terror brought the words tumbling out headlong. He
repented all his sins though he didn't really believe he had any
serious ones; God might have a different scale book. As he prayed,
the weather perversely worsened and the cabin tilted more sharply
than ever, tilted until the bunk appeared to rise above his kneel-
ing body and he slid backwards to fetch up against the door
while things crashed around him, blasted Russians, they never
secured anything in a seamanlike fashion . . . the drawers beneath
the bunk flew open and Russian underwear lay draped across
him. The monkey's skull sped across the compartment and the
thigh bone struck him full in the face.

"Oh, God damn!" he shouted. His last moment had come
and he had hurt his back too. As the cabin resumed its normal
level he glared across at the monkey's skull which, by some
fluke, had shot back the other way and landed on the bunk.
Atop its dreadful grin lay Captain Watkiss's brass-bound cap.

He shut his eyes and trembled. He felt he was dead already
and was looking at his own flesh-bared skull . . .

It had been a long, long night and the dawn was just as bad.
On two occasions during that appalling night the *Talisman* had
broached-to and had come round only by a miracle. After the
first experience the standard compass had gone, smashed by a
wickedly heavy sea that dumped itself down smack on the

bridge. The bridge itself had been left a shambles, as had Number One gun just for'ard of it; and Halfhyde had shifted aft to emergency steering, where he had found the compass unreliable. Soon after this a ferocious sea had swept all his remaining boats from the davits, pounding them to matchwood as they lifted against the superstructure. The skies were utterly impenetrable—no hope whatsoever of a star sight. All Halfhyde could do was to plug on, keeping his bows into wind and seas as best he could.

Soon after what passed for dawn—no more than the faintest lightening of the blackness—Halliburton fought his way aft along the life-lines and approached Halfhyde.

"Well, Mr Halliburton! Damage?"

Halliburton shouted over the scream of the wind. "No basic structural damage below, sir. Nothing that'll affect our seaworthiness. On deck the bridge and the fore gun and the boats—"

"Yes, that much I know! And the torpedo-tubes?"

"All intact, sir, except for—"

"Except for what the last typhoon did!"

"Yes, sir. And at least we're afloat. That's something."

"Casualties?"

"None, sir."

"None at all?"

"No, sir."

"Somebody," Halfhyde said, "has wrought a miracle, Mr Halliburton! I fancy we've been in the hands of God—and I trust He keeps them beneath us until we steam into clear weather! Keep the carpenter's mate sounding round, if you please, and he's to report at once if we make the smallest amount of water below."

"Aye, aye, sir." Halliburton raised a hand to the brim of his streaming sou'wester and turned away, still gripping the life-line as he made his way to the hatch to go below. As he lifted the cover, a sea swept aft from the labouring bows, forcing them under as it thundered along the deck in swirling foam. The first lieutenant was virtually washed down the ladder from the lip of the hatch before the weight of water took the cover from his grip and slammed it shut again behind him. Halfhyde, braced against the rail running at waist level around the after steering position, felt himself lifted up bodily as the big sea raced on aft. Turning to look astern he could see no deck: the water that had lifted him was as one with the sea behind. In spite of the basically undamaged condition of the ship, he still feared for his command. The weather was far from moderating yet; the bottom was still out of the glass and anything could happen.

The wind tugged and battered, the waters swirled. By superhuman efforts the quartermaster kept the ship's head into the wind and sea, and the engine-room kept a full head of steam below—but for how much longer that could be done Halfhyde was unable to say. Already the engineer had reported that his bunkers were low; the extra steaming called for in the typhoon was to blame for that. By this time, in fair weather, they would not have been far off Paravela and would have had bunkers enough to make their arrival. Everything depended now on how long the typhoon lasted.

On the admiral's bridge, Prince Gorsinski stared out into the same appalling conditions. Vast as the *Catherine the Great* was, she was but a minnow in the enormous tracts of raging sea. She laboured horribly, lifted to hang suspended on the crests, then plunged deep in a swooping motion to take the full force of nature on her exposed for'ard guns, which for much of the time were invisible beneath the water as it flung back towards the midships superstructure to smash into heavy spray that reached to the admiral's bridge itself.

Gorsinski scowled.

Reports had been reaching him continually: reports of the ingress of water via hatches and sprung plates, reports of electrical breakdowns in the power supply to the gun-turrets, reports of steam pipes fracturing under the tremendous stresses of the violent movement. Such should not happen; a Russian battleship should be able to withstand the worst that nature could fling at her. There were going to be some heavy punishments if Prince Gorsinski had his way: the naval architects and constructors at the dockyard where the *Catherine the Great* had been laid down and where she had last been refitted—or his own engineers for failing to carry out proper routine maintenance. Shooting would be too easy.

Gorsinski raised his voice. "Flag Captain."

"Yes, Your Highness?"

"My servant. Brandy. The cold is wicked."

"At once, Your Highness."

The urgent message went down. Gorsinski continued staring at the racing seas, heaving through the overcast. The wind screamed around the tall masts and yards like a thousand devils, twanging at the wires and ropes of the rigging like a mad orchestra. The admiral's servant staggered up with a fitted box containing the wherewithal to satisfy his master. Refraining from looking directly at majesty he set the box down and brought out a silver salver, a crystal decanter of brandy, and a glass. Deftly he poured three fingers: he knew Prince Gorsinski's wishes. Gorsinski took the glass from the salver without a word and threw back the contents in a single swallow. He then sent the glass crashing into a corner of the bridge and turned his back on his servant.

"Flag Captain, I sense an improvement. Slight but noticeable—some lifting of the overcast. You agree?"

"Perhaps, Your Highness. Almost imperceptible, but—"

"Perceptible to me."

"Yes, Your Highness."

"I believe we are beginning to be left behind by the typhoon. You will see. I believe the worst is over."

The flag captain nodded without committing himself to speech. He felt his admiral was being over-optimistic; possibly it was the brandy reaching his stomach. However, within the next couple of hours there was an improvement and, although the seas were still immensely high and would remain so for a while yet, there was a slight rise in the barometric pressure and the weight of the wind had lessened. By afternoon the *Catherine the Great* was able to come back to her proper course for Paravela, with her lookouts straining their eyes for a sight of the other ships of the scattered squadron. This was a difficult task; although by this time there had been a considerable lifting of the overcast, the visibility was little more than some three or four cables'-lengths.

Captain Watkiss was more than delighted to be still alive and felt that his improvised prayers had been decently listened to. The cabin was a shambles, but never mind that. It was a mere part of the total shambles into which his life had fallen. God alone could tell what Their Lordships of the Admiralty were going to say eventually about his period on the island, tool of a pair of dreadful renegades, fugitives from justice. Of course, they were dead now, both of them, and Halfhyde would be needed to give vital evidence in his support. Post captains didn't tell lies but the Board of Admiralty was composed of a notoriously unreliable bunch of sea-lawyers, schemers, and persons who had climbed to their pinnacles of power over mounds of broken careers and destroyed reputations, and they'd always been jealous of him in any case. His career might well be over.

Captain Watkiss worried on and seethed in an impotent silence until he heard someone opening his cabin door, by which time he had noted a distinct improvement in the battleship's motion. There was now little more than a roll left; the dreadful pitching, the nasty corkscrew effect, and the sudden lifts and thwacking descents had gone.

A Russian lieutenant stood there, the one who had been appointed in charge of the prisoner. This person smiled and said, "Good morning, Captain." He had a little English, but not much.

"Good morning," Watkiss snapped. "What do you want?"

"The deck, Captain."

"What? I don't understand you."

The Russian sought for words. "Prince Gorsinski, Captain. He—"

"He wishes to speak to me?"

"No, not at all." The lieutenant, blowing out his cheeks, lifted a hand and waggled two fingers along his other arm. The fingers advanced towards his wrist. Watkiss stared. The Russian said, "The walk. You see?"

"Oh, balls and bang-me-arse, exercise! Why the devil didn't you say so in the first place instead of fiddling about with all that damn play-acting!" Watkiss reached for his uniform cap and planted it squarely on his head. "All right, you may go, I know the way to the quarterdeck, thank you."

He emerged with dignity from the cabin, leaving the Russian to shut the door. He bounced along the cabin alleyway, lurching from time to time as the battleship rolled. Reaching the door in the after part of the superstructure, he went through to the open deck. The overcast was still there and there was a swell left behind by the typhoon as it hurried north-westerly across the Pacific. There were no other ships in sight so far as could be seen from aft—neither British nor Russian.

Watkiss suffered a feeling of desertion, but admitted to himself, reluctantly, that to scatter as soon as the storm was imminent was only prudent—Bassinghorn had done the right thing there. It would be a nasty business if two ships should collide in a typhoon.

But what was to happen to him now?

He paced up and down, thinking hard and coming to no conclusions. Then all at once he saw something. It was just a shape, really, in the overcast astern. Nothing much. Watkiss looked intently, screwing up his eyes. It became a little clearer. He was convinced it was a vessel of some sort and that it was overtaking very slowly. He was seaman enough to know that shapes seen indistinctly at sea in poor visibility could be tantalizingly hard to identify and indeed could often be no more than a trick of the imagination. Almost a hallucination.

He didn't believe this one was that. No! It was taking on firmer outlines—and it was small. Not, therefore, one of the blasted dago squadron. Captain Watkiss felt great excitement. If his suspicion was right—if the shape was Halfhyde's torpedo-boat destroyer—then he was being looked for. Or even if it was just coincidence, it would be glorious to see the White Ensign once again.

Knowing that at any moment the emerging ship would be

spotted by the Russian lookouts if it hadn't been already, Captain Watkiss moved aft, hoping that he would be seen from the overtaking vessel's bridge, hoping also that he would not now be removed below before a telescope had picked him up and identified him.

It was Halliburton who was first to recognize the battleship from the after steering position. He said, "It's the *Catherine the Great,* sir, without a doubt."

Halfhyde stared through his telescope. "You may be right, Mr Halliburton, but I can't pick out the admiral's flag yet. I'll wait until I do."

"We'll have it in a moment," Halliburton said. "We're overtaking quite fast."

Within the next five minutes the identification was made for certain. Prince Gorsinski's flag was seen flaunted at the masthead and the moment it was seen a lamp began flashing from the Russian's bridge.

Halfhyde called, "Yeoman!"

"Yessir, reading, sir."

Halfhyde continued staring through his telescope, raking the battleship from stem to stern as he took the *Talisman* in fast on a closing course. His long look was rewarded and he gave a hard laugh. "Mr Halliburton, do you see what I see?"

"What's that, sir?"

"Captain Watkiss—or John Frumm—on the port side of the quarterdeck. He's waving to us. God knows what he expects of us—but I've got a fair idea of what I'm *going* to do, Mr Halliburton!"

"Yes, sir?"

Halfhyde was about to answer when the yeoman of signals

reported, "Message from the Russian Flag, sir: *I congratulate your small ship on its survival. If you do not stand clear I shall turn and ram you.*"

Halfhyde smiled icily. "A kindly gesture indeed! Make from *Talisman: you are too unwieldy to turn as fast as I can.*" He paused. "Mr Halliburton, six hands to the fo'c'sle, starboard side."

"You mean—"

"At the double, if you please—they're to stand by to grapple a heavy weight aboard as soon as it jumps!" Halfhyde bent to the engine-room voice-pipe. "Engine emergency full ahead. Give her all you've got, and stand by to go astern within the next few minutes." He slammed the cover back and began passing the helm orders as the speed increased and the *Talisman* strained forward like a greyhound. He was shaking with impatience to lay his ship alongside the Russian's quarterdeck before his intentions were spotted, before the wretched Watkiss was removed into safe custody, which must happen, surely, at any moment. Overtaking faster now, the *Talisman's* bows raced up towards the battleship's port quarter. The hands detailed by the first lieu-tenant, six of the most reliable seamen ratings, were in position for'ard, standing with difficulty on the turtle-deck and carrying a heavy net between them. As they raced up, Halfhyde saw the startled look on Watkiss's face, saw both the monocle and the goatskin flying out along the wind.

He cupped his hands and shouted, "Jump the moment I'm in position. I'll not be able to linger!"

Watching his helm closely through narrowed eyes, Halfhyde nudged his bows up alongside the battleship's quarterdeck, com-ing past the admiral's stern-walk as he did so. Once in position, with his stem immediately below Captain Watkiss, leaving the latter with a drop of up to ten feet, if he was unlucky in his timing, on to a heaving deck, he put his engines full astern. He drifted a little past, then as the sternway began to bite the *Talisman* steadied to keep pace with the battleship. Halfhyde roared out, *"Now!"*

A shout came from for'ard. "Russians doubling aft, sir!"

His heart in his mouth, Halfhyde waited. From his position aft he was unable to see along the Russian deck: he was too low down, too close to the immense steel side. He saw Watkiss look over his shoulder, saw the lips part in what was probably a yell of fear, then there was a flutter of goatskin and the plump body launched itself into space. In that precise moment an unkindly quirk of the sea, passing beneath the *Talisman's* bottom-plating, lifted her and flung her over to port. Captain Watkiss plummeted clear of the fo'c'sle, slap into the sea. Cursing savagely, Halfhyde did the only thing he could in the interest of not squashing Watkiss as flat as a pancake between his own ship and the Russian: he continued full astern and came clear as a bunch of Russian sailors armed with rifles glared down into the Pacific.

Chapter 13

HALFHYDE lifted clenched fists in the air: he was suffering a high degree of frustration since he had lost all his boats to the typhoon's tearing menace. Unorthodox methods must perforce be tried. "Mr Halliburton, I'm taking my ship back in towards Captain Watkiss, very gently. Get your hands to stand by with grappling irons on the starboard bow. And they'd better lower that net right away."

"Aye, aye sir. I don't like the look of those armed Russians—"

"We'll chance them," Halfhyde said briefly. "Move as fast as God will let you, Mr Halliburton!" The first lieutenant went down at the rush. Halfhyde passed the helm and engine orders to take the *Talisman* ahead to where Watkiss could now be seen, goatskin splayed out and cap gone, looking waterlogged already. But the rescue attempt was to be too late. The *Catherine the Great's* engines lay stopped now, the screws motionless so as to preserve the life of the British captain—someone on the battleship's bridge had reacted with commendable promptness. So had other members of the Russian ship's company: the port quarter guardrail was lined with oilskinned seamen and a rope was going down, followed by another and another, each with a grappling iron at its end. As Halfhyde watched, Captain Watkiss's body took the spiked hooks of two Russian grapnels and there was a yell of pain from the water. Watkiss reached up and grasped the ropes, taking his weight off the hooks, and as he did so an order was called and he was fished bodily from the water, rising fast and dripping like a sponge, banging now and again off the side plating, his features frozen into a look of intense concentration and his eyes staring. There was a roar of unkind laughter from the Russians as the prize catch reached the quarterdeck and collapsed in a sodden heap, gasping for air. The heap was hauled to its feet by two Russian seamen. As he hung like a limp doll from the stalwart arms, Captain Watkiss found his voice and yelled furiously, "You are a blasted nincompoop, Mr Halfhyde, a blasted *nincompoop,* and that's fact— I said it!"

They were back where they had started, but at least they had the Russian under a kind of surveillance now and could use him as perhaps a better guide than an unreliable compass—Halfhyde intended to remain in company all the way to Paravela in spite of sundry threats or hints of threats signalled by Prince Gorsinski. Halfhyde was still much concerned about his bunkers, and could only hope he would have enough to reach Paravela, as he remarked to his first lieutenant.

"What happens about Captain Watkiss," Halliburton asked anxiously, "when we reach there?"

"We shall see," was all Halfhyde said, enigmatically. In all honesty he was flummoxed. As a Japanese possession Paravela owed no allegiance to Queen Victoria, and there would be no Residency to which to refer the matter of Watkiss's captivity. The Japanese would all too probably prove unhelpful. It was anyone's guess as to which side they would come down on if they were approached for assistance. Meanwhile the weather continued to moderate and at noon Halfhyde was able to fix the ship's position by sun sight beneath a clear sky: he found he was not so far off Paravela. The sea itself remained restless and there was a heavy swell; the two ships rolled badly. Halfhyde maintained station off the port quarter of the Russian battleship. There was no further exchange of signals and there was no further sight of Captain Watkiss, who was presumably now confined below-decks, a person no longer to be trusted with his liberty. Halfhyde grinned to himself as he thought about Watkiss, who had always been inclined to a strong degree of prickliness when forced to take orders even from British admirals. Captain Watkiss, a poor subordinate, would make a fiendish prisoner-of-war.

As the sun shone down Halfhyde, who had already made a detailed examination of the ship below-decks, accompanied his first lieutenant for'ard to take stock of the damaged bridge and Number One gun. The carpenter's mate and his party were working on the bridge and the main steering gear: they would be able to effect running repairs and the bridge would be usable again, but the gun, like the torpedo-tube damaged in the first typhoon, would be a job for the dockyard at Hong Kong. Having inspected the bridge, Halfhyde made his way aft to the torpedo-tubes, where he had a word with the torpedo-gunner.

"Well, Mr Stallybrass, you're still our first line of attack, it seems."

"Aye, sir, I am that!"

Halfhyde smiled. "Try not to be over eager, Mr Stallybrass. The look in your eye says you'd like nothing better than to loose your torpedoes against the Russian—but that would be likely to sink Captain Watkiss as well!"

Prince Gorsinski was conferring with his flag captain; the latter had expressed doubts about their forthcoming sojourn in the island of Paravela. For a certainty the British would make representations about the capture and abduction of Captain Watkiss.

"No doubt," Gorsinski agreed. "But that is as far as it will go, Flag Captain."

"You sound very sure, Your Highness."

Gorsinski laughed. "I am sure. Vice-Admiral Nishimura is in Paravela with a cruiser squadron. The Japanese are not friendly towards us—that is true. But Vice-Admiral Nishimura will prove helpful. I was once of some service to him—a rescue at sea. He will not forget that, but if he does, then there are other methods. Nishimura has a kinsman, a cousin who means much to him, imprisoned in Siberia—a case of espionage in which His Imperial Majesty exercised clemency. A word from me to His Imperial Majesty and the clemency will be withdrawn and the cousin will die. That is the way the world goes, Flag Captain— and Nishimura is a man of the world! I shall not even be put to the distasteful business of mentioning the matter—you will see. Now, to the person of Captain Watkiss himself."

"Yes, Your Highness?"

Gorsinski stretched himself and yawned; he was tired after much bridge-keeping and his sea cabin was small and claustrophobic. As he stretched, his longs legs abutted against his chest-of-drawers. He said, "As a matter of prudence, the good captain must be concealed whilst we are coaling, and indeed until we leave for the islands where he is to begin his work. He may be looked for."

"But if your influence with Vice-Admiral Nishimura is effective, Your Highness—"

"We must respect Nishimura's personal position, Flag Captain. He will put in a word, but he must not be seen to interfere too obviously. If the British complain, as complain they will, the port authorities must be seen to act—to search my flagship. Nishimura may not be able to prevent that. If not, then he will be relying upon *us,* my dear fellow, to ensure that any search is fruitless, do you not understand?"

The flag captain nodded. "Yes, Your Highness."

"Good! Now—the place of concealment. And what better than to borrow a stratagem of the wretched Lieutenant Halfhyde's, which he once used against me in Sevastopol?" Gorsinski laughed again, in high good humour. "The fellow will be hoist with his own petard and will be made a monkey of! Now, just listen very carefully, Flag Captain . . ."

Early the following morning the *Catherine the Great's* navigating officer made his landfall off Paravela and duly reported to the flag captain and the admiral. Still in company, Halfhyde also made his landfall. As the two ships approached more closely, a Japanese squadron was identified lying off the island and a number of masts and fighting-tops were seen in the harbour. Halfhyde was soon able to identify the *Port Royal,* which was already occupying one of the coaling berths. Astern of her lay the *Plantagenet,* also busily taking bunkers beneath a filthy cloud of coal-dust.

"We're together again as a squadron, Mr Halliburton," Halfhyde remarked. A moment later the yeoman of signals saluted and reported a message.

"From the commodore, sir. You are to repair aboard immediately on berthing astern of *Plantagenet.*"

Halfhyde nodded, then looked across at the *Catherine the Great,* which had now reduced speed for entering the lagoon. There was no sign of the *Smolensk* though the *Berezina* was in the lagoon and swinging to her starboard anchor. Halfhyde reflected upon the empty coaling berth, standing ready to receive him while the Russian waited; that must indicate not only an insistence on the part of Bassinghorn, but also a degree of co-operation with the British Navy on the part of the Japanese port authorities. That gave hope. The day was brightening in more ways than one and Halfhyde took the *Talisman* inwards on a surge of optimism.

Across the water and now a little astern of the *Talisman*, the gloom of Captain Watkiss had deepened even further. He had felt far from well ever since his immersion in the South Pacific; the sudden fall had shaken him up. The flagship's doctor had attended him and he had been well enough treated, but leeches were leeches whatever their nationality and seemed to think they knew better than he did about his own body; besides, the indignity of his sudden descent rankled and was upsetting to his constitution. There was no cause for optimism as to his future, either: he was about to be evacuated from his temporary quarters under Prince Gorsinski's orders. His next location was being explained to him by the pidgin-English-speaking lieutenant who was doing his best in difficult circumstances.

"Anonymity, Captain. The admiral wishes this, you understand."

"I don't understand at all and I consider it blasted cheek. I am a post captain in Her Majesty's Fleet and am not to be trifled with." Captain Watkiss took a deep breath and blew it out again. His face was red with fury. He disliked being anonymous and he was damned if he was going to be. To dress him up as a Russian rating, to fall him in with the common herd, to berth him in the seamen's mess deck, was quite intolerable; but he would comply because it was obvious he was going to have to. That, however, was as far as he would go. Anonymity would not be granted to the Russians whatever they might think. It was to be presumed that after Bassinghorn had made his damning report of the Russian atrocity, the authorities would search the ship . . . which was why the blasted Russians wanted him to be anonymous, of course, but if they fancied he could be fooled, then more fools them! He had seen through it instantly . . . and the moment any person from the shore appeared within range of him, he would yell the place down, establish his identity, and that would be that.

Or would it?

The Russian lieutenant had more to say.

"If there is trouble . . . if there is vocal sound, yes? Then more trouble will come for you, Captain, I am sorry."

Watkiss glared and heaved his goatskin into a more comfortable position across his shoulders. "What do you mean?"

"A sound, Captain, and a strong, big man will strike you down instantly and you will be carried off."

Captain Watkiss's mouth opened, then shut again. His face became purple and he gasped. Words failed him. *The buggers!* He didn't doubt that they would do it; the Russians were known to be dreadful people, bullies, murderers—free use of belaying-pins and the iron-hard fists of the petty officers. Aboard a Russian ship no port authority would ever query the manhandling of a common seaman. Speech returned and Watkiss uttered angrily. He said, "You're a set of damn cads and bounders!"

"Your pardon, Captain?"

"Oh, hold your tongue."

Halfhyde walked along the jetty as the Long Range Squadron coaled ship. The morning was hot, the sky clear; the only traces of the typhoon were the shoreside effects—the storm-damaged buildings, the littered state of the berths, trees flattened to the ground behind the jetties. The harbour was a primitive one and the port offices and stores had been no more than wooden huts. There were few left intact; collapsed walls and roofs lay beneath a patina of coal-dust. By the time Halfhyde reached the *Port Royal's* brow his white uniform was already filthy. Commodore Bassinghorn, when Halfhyde was taken to his quarters, was more sensibly clad in an old pair of white duck trousers and a worn-out monkey-jacket. Coal-dust, as was the way when coaling ship, had penetrated everywhere below and the commodore's quarters were not immune.

"Foul business," Bassinghorn said. "I would I could return to the good, clean days of sail!"

"Yes, indeed, sir." Bidden to a chair, Halfhyde sat. "Have you news of Captain Watkiss, by any chance?"

Bassinghorn shook his head sombrely. "None. I take it he's still aboard the Russian?"

"He is, sir." Halfhyde reported briefly on his abortive attempt at getting Watkiss away from the *Catherine the Great,* and then asked, "Do you propose to ask the assistance of the port authorities, sir?"

"For what it may be worth, I have already done so."

"With little result?"

"I believe they may make a search, but I'm not hopeful. All the same, the formalities had to be observed."

"Protocol is all," Halfhyde murmured. "Yes, I concede it had to be tried, sir. And when it fails . . . then will come the time for unorthodox methods."

"Unorthodox methods?"

Halfhyde said, "I shall be thinking, sir. Some stratagem is called for—or will be called for shortly." He paused, and met

Bassinghorn's eye squarely. "If I were to act upon my own initiative, sir, without necessarily finding a need to inform you first, then any subsequent strictures would go no higher than myself."

Bassinghorn frowned. He said coldly, "I stand in no need of taking shelter behind junior lieutenants, Halfhyde."

"I'm sorry, sir—"

"I appreciate your thought, but you will take no action whatsoever without my sanction. If that sanction is given, I and I alone shall take the responsibility. Is that understood?"

"Yes, sir," Halfhyde answered. He had been given the reply he had expected and from now on there would be no doubt that anything he might do on his own would be a breach of expressed orders from the commodore and Bassinghorn's yard-arm would be clear vis-à-vis the Admiralty. That was as he wished it. Halfhyde had an immense respect and liking for Henry Bassinghorn, and Bassinghorn had more to lose than a junior lieutenant if matters should go awry under his command. Better that he should be by-passed by some subterfuge, some unofficial act without his knowledge or consent. Halfhyde was philosophic as to his own standing with the Board of Admiralty: he had offended Their Lordships often enough in the past to have lost some of his awe of their edicts. Providing that one's disobedience was attended by a successful result, it was always satisfactory to cock a snook at the Board of Admiralty . . .

Outside the harbour Vice-Admiral Nishimura's cruiser squadron lay peacefully with steam on the main engines to keep the ships in position, flaunting the blood-red rays of the Japanese sun from the ensigns. The ships were clean of the coal-dust that had afflicted them whilst taking bunkers earlier, and snow-white scrubbed canvas awnings had been rigged. Vice-Admiral

Nishimura, a squat man of about the same build as Captain Watkiss, was taking his ease upon the quarterdeck of his flagship, the *Tsuyama,* seated in a deck chair and reflecting upon the sadly distant beauties of a young wife in Yokohama, a young wife with the smallest feet in all Japan. The vice-admiral was not pleased when a steam picket-boat was reported approaching from the harbour, wearing the flag of Admiral Prince Gorsinski; nevertheless politeness was all and Vice-Admiral Nishimura was present in person at his starboard quarterdeck ladder to greet his distinguished visitor.

He smiled ingratiatingly. "Most honoured. Most welcome. Greetings to the Czar of all the Russias." English was being spoken; Gorsinski had no Japanese, Nishimura no Russian. Prince Gorsinski responded with greetings to the Emperor of Japan and indicated that his business was confidential. Casting a regretful look at his empty deck chair, Vice-Admiral Nishimura led the way to his quarters in the stern. Bending his tall body as he walked along the alleyways below, Gorsinski silently cursed small men who built ships with low deckheads. Vice-Admiral Nishimura was, in his view, and especially from behind, more toad than man and Gorsinski disliked being a supplicant in any case. In the vice-admiral's day-cabin he came straight to the point.

"I have a favour to ask, Admiral."

Teeth showed in a grin. "Most honoured to assist."

"Thank you. The matter is simple. As a result of a request from the British commodore, the port authorities wish to search my flagship."

"What reason given, Your Highness?"

"It is suspected that I have a British naval officer aboard."

There was another grin. "You have not?"

"I have not."

The third grin was one of understanding: lies were being told. Nishimura said, "Most honoured to assist where possible."

"I am grateful," Gorsinski said, sounding lofty. "You may assist by ensuring that the port authorities do not in fact carry out a search—you shall tell them that, please. My Czar would not wish a search of his ships in a—in a foreign port."

"Most sorry," Nishimura said, still grinning. "Cannot interfere with port authorities."

Gorsinski had in fact expected this. He said, "As a fellow admiral, I understand that, naturally. But you will have much influence with the port authorities, who will respect your views and wishes."

"Yes."

"Then if a search must be made I ask that you ensure not too penetrating a disturbance. A word in the ear of the person in charge—I think you understand?"

"The British officer, you do not wish him found?"

"There *is* no British officer," Gorsinski said coldly.

"Yes. Then he will not in any case be found."

Gorsinski breathed hard down his nose. The yellow man was a fool; certain things needed not to be said. Nishimura's grin did not waver. He went on, "The British officer is not existing. If he were, who would he be? For assistance, I must know."

It was no use; Nishimura was adamant. He held the whip-hand for the moment. Gorsinski said, "One Watkiss, a post captain of the British Fleet. It is he whom the British think is aboard my ship."

"And he is not."

"He is not."

The same lie again. Nishimura said flatly, "Most sorry, cannot assist. Have own position to consider."

"But I think you—"

"Most sorry."

Vice-Admiral Nishimura was more adamant than ever.
Gorsinski's lower jaw came out threateningly. Something he had
intended not to raise would have to be mentioned after all. In
a harsh voice he said, "You must have a care, Admiral, for the
well-being of your cousin in Siberia. I think I need say no more?"

It seemed impossible to extinguish the grin. There was a
lengthy pause then Nishimura said, "Most clear. But to me
another thing is also most clear."

"What?"

Nishimura gave a small bow and for a space the grin was
not seen. He said, "The Captain Watkiss who is not aboard your
flagship will be removed from where he is not by the port
authorities, and he will not be returned until kinsman is released
from Siberia." The grin became wider. "Most honoured boot is
on other foot."

Chapter 14

"CAPTAIN, SIR?"

"Yes, Mr Halliburton?"

"Prince Gorsinski's not returned from the Japanese squadron, sir—his picket-boat has, but he wasn't aboard."

Halfhyde stared. "You're sure?"

"Quite sure, sir. There was a good deal of consternation on the Russian quarterdeck when the midshipman reported back aboard."

Halfhyde got to his feet and left his cabin. With Halliburton he climbed to the upper deck and levelled his telescope on the *Catherine the Great*. There seemed to be shouting and arm-waving; the flag captain and the battleship's commander were there with a number of other officers. The wretched midshipman of the picket-boat was still being harangued. Halfhyde lowered his telescope. "Something is up," he said. "It looks as though Gorsinski may have been detained aboard the Japanese flagship. If so, I wish I knew why!"

"Something to do with Captain Watkiss, sir?"

"It's possible. But why? Why detain Gorsinski, for heaven's sake?" Halfhyde paced the deck, frowning. Gorsinski was clearly up to some kind of jiggery-pokery; why pay a visit to the Japanese in the first place? Courtesy? Perhaps, perhaps not. More likely chicanery—the Japanese and the Russians didn't normally hobnob much. If it was chicanery, who could it concern but Captain Watkiss?

Who indeed?

Halfhyde turned to his first lieutenant. "I'm going aboard the *Port Royal*," he said. "I'll not be long. I want all possible speed in completing bunkering, and I shall want steam by the time we've finished."

"Aye, aye, sir." Halliburton paused. "Do you mean to go to sea, sir?"

"I want to be ready to do so. There's dirty work going on— it's possible Watkiss was removed temporarily to the Japanese squadron in Gorsinski's picket-boat, and Gorsinski intends transferring him back to his own flagship at sea. If that's the case, I shall put a spoke in his wheel, Mr Halliburton." As he turned away Halliburton put a hand on his sleeve.

"Sir—"

"What is it?"

"A boat going off from the shore, sir, towards the Russian flagship."

Halliburton pointed and Halfhyde brought up his telescope again. A steamboat was heading out, crammed to the gunwhales with armed Japanese soldiers. In the after cockpit stood a little man in civilian dress looking pompously important as he stared towards the *Catherine the Great* and its powerful guns.

It had all happened just as predicted by the Russian lieutenant: Captain Watkiss found himself fallen in with the common seamen, dressed in a common seaman's appalling rig which stank of its previous tenant. Watkiss was herded this way and that to incomprehensible Russian orders, ferociously yelled out by a petty officer and accompanied by the all too frequent use of a tarred rope's-end which smote him on the shoulders, on the arms, on the buttocks. The indignity was as appalling as the pain. The mess deck where he was fallen in smelled strongly of unwashed bodies, of foul stockings and stale food, a foetid atmosphere that could be cut with a knife. Life was torture. After an agonizing interval, soldiers came with rifles and bayonets and, although they were only Japanese, Captain Watkiss knew that his moment, if it was to come at all, had come now. It was very plain that he was being sought, so he took the risk of announcing himself, or trying to. The moment he uttered his first syllable the "strong, big man" behind him went into action and he was thrown to the deck and sat upon by two men, one of them placing his rump on his captive's face. Speech, even breathing, was now impossible. Captain Watkiss struck out with his legs, which were immediately pinioned.

This, he believed, was when he should have been dragged away into anonymity, but something must have gone wrong. An order was given, the soldiers made a bee-line for the scene of the struggle and a small civilian began shouting almost hysterically—typical, Watkiss thought, of a Japanese, blasted foreigners the lot of them . . . but he had managed against all odds to make his point so all was well. As, under the orders apparently of the civilian, he was hoisted to his feet, he said breathlessly, "I am not a damn Russian, I am Captain Watkiss of—"

"Yes. You will come."

"Thank you. It's about blasted time." Watkiss shook himself free of the Russians. "I should have thought you'd have acted sooner than this, you know. Much sooner. But what can one expect of dagoes? I suppose I'm lucky you've come at all. What's the meaning of this?" he added in alarm as two of the soldiers seized his arms and forced him along the mess deck.

"You are being made to come," the civilian said.

"It's quite unnecessary." The soldiers were moving fast and Watkiss's short legs twinkled rapidly. *"Will you kindly let go of me, blast you!"*

"Will not let go."

A great fear gripping him now, Captain Watkiss was propelled to the upper deck and down the accommodation-ladder into a steamboat still clad in his Russian seaman's gear. He protested that he wished to go ashore dressed as an officer; the Japanese took no notice. The boat was borne off the side of the *Catherine the Great* and headed, not for the shore, but out of the harbour entrance towards the open sea.

Halfhyde was aboard the *Port Royal* for longer than he had expected; Bassinghorn was engaged ashore with the port authorities, making further representations in regard to Captain Watkiss, and it was some while before he returned aboard. He was much alarmed at Halfhyde's news of Gorsinski and agreed that the Japanese squadron should be watched as discreetly as possible.

"No stratagems?" he asked.

"None as yet, sir."

"Keep your enthusiasm under full control, Halfhyde."

"Of course, sir." Halfhyde took his leave and walked back along the coaling jetty to the *Talisman,* where the operation of bunkering was now complete. The first lieutenant had already done a good job with the wash-deck hoses and the ship was becoming nicely clean.

"And Prince Gorsinski?" Halfhyde asked.

"He's not returned, sir. The Japanese shoreside boat has left the flagship—"

"So I see."

"It appeared to take a Russian rating with it, sir, and then to head seawards."

"A rating? And to seaward?" Halfhyde's voice was cold. "What did this rating look like, Mr Halliburton?"

"Just like any other rating, I would say, sir—"

"And I would say that it's possible he was Captain Watkiss disguised as a rating, Mr Halliburton! How long ago did this take place?"

"No more than ten minutes past, sir."

"I should have been informed immediately, Mr Halliburton, by runner to the *Port Royal*—however, we'll not go into that now. Pipe special sea dutymen, if you please, and secure the ship for sea. Have we steam?"

"Yes, sir." Halliburton gave a cough. "The commodore, sir. Do you wish to make a signal, asking permission for—"

Halfhyde said, "I wish no such thing. The commodore has already agreed that the Japanese should be watched." His tongue was in his cheek; that agreement was about to be stretched to the limit, for which he would take full responsibility afterwards. He started for'ard. "We leave immediately, Mr Halliburton. Send for Mr Stallybrass. He's to report to me on the bridge."

The *Talisman* left harbour within the next ten minutes, by this time twenty minutes behind the Japanese boat, pursued by signals of enquiry from the *Port Royal*, signals that Halfhyde chose to ignore. The TBD came clear of the reef just in time to see the steamboat making alongside the *Tsuyama*. Halfhyde's telescope showed two things: first, that the *Tsuyama* already had way upon her—she was moving at dead slow ahead; second, that a man was being lifted aboard from the steamboat by the whip of a small derrick. The man, in what appeared to be rating's rig, bore a strong resemblance to Captain Watkiss. As the man reached the *Tsuyama's* upper deck, another person, who had been standing by, brandished a fist in his face and was then seized by two Japanese seamen who placed a rope beneath his arms. Gesticulating, this person was hoisted by the whip until he was clear of the cruiser's guardrail and then lowered swiftly into the boat which immediately turned away for the island. Maintaining her course ahead, the *Tsuyama* increased speed.

Halfhyde closed his telescope with a snap. "That," he said, "was Prince Gorsinski or I'm a Dutchman! Mr Halliburton, hands to stand by aft. I'm going alongside the Japanese boat and I want Gorsinski brought aboard. He might come in handy."

"There'll be opposition, sir—"

"Yes, Mr Halliburton, I'm aware of that. It's to be overcome. You will station a guard of seamen on the quarterdeck, with rifles. They're not to be used unless I give the order personally, but they'll make a nice threat." Halfhyde brought up his telescope again and studied the steamboat closely. There was no doubt in his mind that the discharged person was Prince Gorsinski, though currently he was invisible in the cabin. Halliburton saluted and left the bridge and a moment later the boatswain's calls sounded throughout the ship. Men went aft at the double as Halfhyde passed the helm orders to take the *Talisman* across the Japanese boat's course. The latter twisted and turned in an effort to avoid the British warship but she hadn't a chance. Skilfully, Halfhyde laid his command alongside the boat and called from his bridge.

"Down there! You'll put out boathooks and hold yourself to my port quarter. You will then bring out Prince Gorsinski."

There was a confused babble from the Japanese crew, a babble that ceased when Halfhyde called down again. "I shall brook no argument. If there is any trouble I shall open fire." He turned and called aft. "Mr Halliburton!"

The first lieutenant looked up. "Sir?"

"A volley over their heads, if you please. A *close* volley."

"Aye, aye, sir." Halliburton passed the order to the gunner's mate and the rifles crashed out. Aboard the boat, the crew ducked in much alarm and there was more excited shouting; but the point had been made. As the way came off the *Talisman* the Japanese brought up their boathooks and grappled alongside the torpedo-boat destroyer, holding their boat steady. Gorsinski appeared, looking furious. He shook a fist towards the *Talisman's* bridge.

"You shall pay for this, Lieutenant Halfhyde!" he shouted. "I shall demand that you are handed over to accompany me back to Russia and—"

"You're in no position to make demands, sir," Halfhyde called down. "You will come aboard immediately or I shall send down seamen to bring you with force. Mr Halliburton?"

"Sir?"

"You will aim the rifles into the boat."

"Aye, aye, sir!" The reloaded rifles were brought up and their barrels depressed until the mouths stared down at Gorsinski and the Japanese.

"I shall count to twenty," Halfhyde called. "Twenty seconds only." He brought out his watch and began to count. Someone among the Japanese had enough English to reckon the score for himself and pass it on. There was consternation on the Japanese faces and more shouting on a high note. There was a movement towards Gorsinski: they couldn't wait to get rid of him now. The British were unpredictable but were inclined to back their threats, and they regarded all other races as their inferiors. That made them smugly certain of themselves. As a British seaman, at a word from the first lieutenant, was sent down a Jacob's ladder Prince Gorsinski was manhandled towards it by a bunch of babbling Japanese. When he hesitated the boat's skipper produced a nasty-looking curved dagger, pushed through the mob behind Gorsinski, and laid the blade at the Russian's throat. Evidently Gorsinski read the determination in the eyes: furiously he reached out for the Jacob's ladder and swung himself on to it.

He climbed; the boat from the shore lost no time in standing clear, its single screw churning up the water. As Gorsinski stepped aboard the *Talisman*, looking as arrogant as ever, he was met by a piping party and the first lieutenant's smart salute. Contemptuously he kept his hands at his sides.

"Take me to your commanding officer," he said. "At once!"

Halliburton grinned. "At once it shall be, sir." He turned for'ard and made for the bridge, followed by Prince Gorsinski. Already the *Talisman* had way upon her again and was turning in pursuit of the *Tsuyama*. As Gorsinski reached the bridge the ship was shaking throughout her plates in response to full power from the engine-room.

"This is an act of war," Gorsinski stated loudly, "and will be treated as such by my Czar. I think I see the end of your career, Lieutenant Halfhyde!"

Halfhyde shrugged. "It's in the lap of the gods, Your Highness. It's possible I've prevented a war rather than caused one—at least, so far as your Czar is concerned. The Emperor of Japan may find a different situation, perhaps." He paused. "Tell me, sir: do you confirm that Captain Watkiss is aboard the *Tsuyama?*"

"Yes!" Gorsinski snapped. "Perhaps you will tell me what your intentions are?"

"In regard to Captain Watkiss? Why, to snatch him back, of course! He is a valuable property in the eyes of Queen Victoria—"

"I take leave to doubt that," Gorsinski said sneeringly.

Halfhyde smiled. "You do not doubt his value as John Frumm, I believe, sir. I think your schemes in that direction have come adrift. Admiral Nishimura appears to have outwitted you, but by God he's not going to outwit me or out-sail me either!" Halfhyde turned away, hands clasped behind his back. Over his shoulder he said, "You have the freedom of my decks, Your Highness, but you will be most carefully watched until I return to port."

He stepped across to the other side of his navigating bridge and levelled his telescope on the Japanese cruiser. Already Admiral Nishimura was being overtaken; like a greyhound the *Talisman* leaped ahead, throwing back a creamy bow wave as her stem cut through the blue waters of the Pacific to send the sea back into her rushing, tumbling wake. The wind made by her passage whistled through the rigging, the smoke from her three funnels lay as a flattened black band streaming astern. Halfhyde frowned thoughtfully as he looked back at the thick smoke. He banged a fist on the guardrail. Smoke could be made good use of, and in its cover the torpedo-gunner would find fulfilment. Halfhyde caught the warrant officer's eye.

"You've had a long wait, Mr Stallybrass," he said, "but you shall not have much longer!"

•   •   •

"I have nothing to say to you, my dear sir, nothing at all," Captain Watkiss announced. His tone was distant; he was trying to keep a cool head and trying to be polite, since it could pay off, but it was a hard task. The Japanese were quite impossible and they all had bad teeth and thus foul breath. Admiral Nishimura's teeth were pitch black, a revolting sight. Watkiss did his best to avoid looking at them but there was a horrible fascination that continually drew his eyes to the grinning mouth confronting him across the admiral's day-cabin.

"Most sorry you do not speak, Captain. Most sorry not to learn truth."

Watkiss made no response but sat with his arms folded across his stomach, glaring. He felt at an immense disadvantage in his Russian seaman's rig; this was not improving his temper, which was worsening fast in any case as the squat Japanese probed on and on.

"Most sorry not to learn truth," Nishimura proceeded painstakingly, "of why Prince Gorsinski needs you."

"Ask him, then," Watkiss said in a crushing tone. "Send him a signal."

"Will not say."

"Then why didn't you keep him aboard until he *did* say?"

"Most foolish to do so. Russian Prince."

"And what about me, may I ask? I am *British*, as you're well aware, Prince or not. Why keep *me* aboard?" Captain Watkiss was working himself up fast. "The British are a damn sight more to be feared by your blasted Emperor—"

"Please—"

"Oh, hold your tongue. The British, as I was saying, are more to be feared than the Russians and that's fact—I said it. Yet you let Gorsinski go and keep me. You're all the same, you blasted dagoes, no common sense. But you'll learn—you'll learn! If you don't put me aboard the *Talisman* this instant, why, you'll be taught a lesson you'll not forget, you stupid little bugger—"

"Most sorry. Much waste of breath." Nishimura seemed imperturbable, either a sponge for insults or not having quite enough colloquial English to appreciate them. "In the meantime, most honoured by presence of British officer, who will go back in time. You like tea?"

"No."

"Most sorry. Japanese custom, very nice."

Watkiss seethed. Damn the tea, he could do with a gin, but he certainly wasn't going to ask. Things were getting worse than ever; he had no idea where he was bound or what the blasted dagoes meant to do with him. When he had been on deck he had seen the *Talisman* turning to follow, but since then he had had no availability of information as to the TBD's movements. It was all up to Halfhyde now, and God alone could say what Halfhyde intended to do, if anything. However, to have him near—if he was still near—brought some comfort. Just a crumb. Halfhyde was unpredictable and it was unfortunate that he, Watkiss, had been surly towards him in the past. But Halfhyde had always been loyal, and surely would never allow his former captain to remain in hostile hands. If only he could go out on deck he would be prepared to risk another descent into the sea; but such had been forbidden by order of the horrible little squat toad who was now ringing for his wretched tea.

"The time has come," Halfhyde said, "to make a signal. Yeoman?"

"Yessir?"

"Make to Vice-Admiral Nishimura from *Talisman: I request you to stop engines and transfer Captain Watkiss to me immediately.*"

"Aye, aye, sir."

The signal was clicked out on an Aldis lamp, and duly acknowledged. Then there was a lengthy delay. Halfhyde paced his bridge, back and forth, hands clasped behind his back, growing impatient. He was close off the *Tsuyama*'s starboard quarter now, maintaining the same speed as the cruiser but with many additional knots in hand should he wish to overtake. Ideas chased one another through his head: it might just be possible to act as a sheepdog, to herd the *Tsuyama*: turn her and chivvy her back towards Paravela, still not very distant. It would be a risk, of course; Nishimura might decide to cut straight through him with his heavy stem. The *Talisman* would go down like a stone. There had to be a better stratagem than that . . .

"Jap signalling, sir." The yeoman read off the *Tsuyama*'s lamp and reported: "*Most regretfully cannot grant request,* sir."

Halfhyde nodded. "Make: *I now feel free to act in accordance with general Admiralty Instructions to safeguard Royal Naval personnel.*" He grinned. "We'll see what Nishimura makes of that! Mr Stallybrass?"

"Sir?"

"Man your torpedo-tube and lay it upon the *Tsuyama*."

"Aye, aye, sir!" Mr Stallybrass saluted and went down the ladder as fast as his portly frame would allow. Halfhyde moved to the engine-room voice-pipe and blew down it. The engineer answered.

"Start closing your dampers," Halfhyde ordered. "I want to make smoke—plenty of it, and thick." He banged down the voice-pipe cover and turned to his first lieutenant, his decision now made. "Mr Halliburton, I intend to beard the Japanese dragon in his own den."

Halliburton looked bewildered.

"I intend to board," Halfhyde said calmly. "Myself, with a dozen seamen under the gunner's mate—to the rescue of Captain Watkiss. We shall all be armed with cutlasses, in the tradition of Lord Nelson. I shall hand over the ship to you, Mr Halliburton, within the next few minutes, and you will close the *Tsuyama* under cover of our smokescreen which by that time I shall have laid ahead. You understand?"

Halliburton was looking dazed. "Yes, sir, but—"

"No buts, Mr Halliburton. I have every confidence in you, be sure of that. You will put the ship as close as possible to the cruiser's quarterdeck on the starboard side, and we shall jump through the smoke. After that, you will take her clear for firing off torpedoes. Now, pipe for the gunner's mate and have a boarding party detailed immediately."

As the boatswain's call started shrilling, Halfhyde looked aft at his funnels. Already the smoke was thickening into heavy black as the dampers cut the air supply to the coal in the furnaces. Halfhyde called down to the torpedo-gunner in the waist, passing further orders. Stallybrass was to be ready to send off his torpedoes after the boarding party was across. Mr Halliburton, he said, would give the word to fire if and when it became necessary. As the smoke continued to thicken, Halfhyde passed the helm and engine orders to take the *Talisman* well ahead of the *Tsuyama*. Within the next few minutes, thick, greasy, black clouds swept down over the cruiser as she steamed into the smokescreen, muck that hung heavily over and about her decks. The consternation on the faces of the Japanese could be seen before they vanished in the smoke. By this time the men of the boarding party were mustering with hastily-issued cutlasses, their faces devilish in the smoke that swirled over the *Talisman* as Halfhyde began to drop the ship astern to manoeuvre into position for boarding. A moment later he handed over to the first lieutenant. He said, "You'll not find it easy to keep the *Tsuyama* in view from here, Mr Halliburton, but I shall pass back guidance from the bows. The moment I shout that we're all across, you'll take the ship off to starboard and stand clear at a safe distance."

"Aye, aye, sir. And the attack orders—the torpedoes?"

Halfhyde wiped a hand over his face. He was black with the smoke already. "You will give the order to fire in fifteen minutes from the time you hear my shout, unless a signal is made from the *Tsuyama*—by that time she should be clear of the smoke." The *Tsuyama* was currently still steaming right into the widespread pall of smoke ahead, and the after part of the cruiser lay in concentrated thickness as the *Talisman's* funnels continued their discharge over her decks. Halfhyde said, "I'm banking on it that the torpedoes won't be needed—banking and praying. But if they are, you'll ensure that Mr Stallybrass aims to bring her down by the bows rather than to blow her up." He smiled thinly. "I have a sensible regard for my life and that of Captain Watkiss, to say nothing of my boarding party."

"Yes, sir."

Now the time had come. Halfhyde said, "She's all yours, Mr Halliburton. Do your best."

He left the bridge and went for'ard fast to join the gunner's mate and the men of the boarding party. He passed his simple orders: they were to keep together and be ready to react instantly to his commands as the situation developed. Then, standing poised by the guardrail, he watched for his moment to jump across as the *Talisman's* bows, to his shouted directions, were laid close to the cruiser by the first lieutenant.

•   •   •

They came through the smoke like demons out of hell, waving
their cutlasses as they took the cruiser's quarterdeck, all of them
making it in safety and without injury except for one man with
a broken ankle who had thereafter to be helped along by his
mates. Earlier, bugles had been heard from the cruiser: the guns
were seen to be manned as Halfhyde's party ran forward and the
bows of the *Talisman* pulled away. The Japanese gunners stared
in amazement as the British seamen appeared. At first there was
no reaction, then a petty officer came from behind a gun-shield
with a revolver in his hand.

He fired.

The bullet whistled past Halfhyde's cheek, giving it a graze.
Blood trickled down to his collar. He ran ahead and closed with
the petty officer, got an arm about the man's body and his cutlass at his neck.

He said, "Take me to your admiral. At once!" As more seamen appeared he shouted, "If there is any interference, this man
will die instantly." His gestures, if not his words, appeared to
penetrate. He went aft, clutching the petty officer, the men of
the boarding party backing up close behind, holding their cutlasses menacingly towards the Japanese seamen. By this time the
smoke was clearing; the *Tsuyama,* still moving ahead, was coming out of the laid smokescreen. The full outlines of the cruiser
were seen; also seen was Vice-Admiral Nishimura, staring down
from his bridge, his face just visible over the canvas dodger.

A stream of excited orders came down and more faces joined
that of the admiral. Then the faces were lost to sight as Halfhyde
and his captive petty officer entered the fore superstructure and
began the climb to the admiral's bridge, leaving the boarding

party to block the way behind them. From time to time, as the ladder emerged into the open between the wedding-cake layers of platforms, Halfhyde was able to snatch a sight of the *Talisman,* now in her firing position a little ahead of the cruiser's starboard bow. Halliburton was doing well. Yellow faces stared as Halfhyde passed but there was no interference. As he came out upon the admiral's bridge, Nishimura advanced angrily.

"Most outrageous! What is explanation, please?"

"I've come for Captain Watkiss," Halfhyde said, his arm still holding his hostage tightly and the cutlass ready to slice into the neck; the man was shaking with terror. "You will make him available at once if you don't want your ship to be blown out of the water."

"That is nonsense. A tiny tub! You are under arrest! Tub will be sunk if—"

"Not so fast," Halfhyde said loudly. "If you open fire you may well hit my ship, but you may not. What is certain is that the moment you look like going into action, my torpedo-gunner will send off his torpedoes—and you're a target he can't miss."

"Most stupid. I shall turn towards your ship, between the torpedo trails, and ram."

Halfhyde gave an insulting laugh. "At this range? You haven't the time or space, Admiral, and you know it!"

Nishimura turned to look; he scowled. He stared at Halfhyde: Halfhyde put all his determination into his features as he stared back unwaveringly. It was Nishimura who looked away.

Halfhyde said, "It's not an empty threat, Admiral, believe me. I am acting for the honour of my country, of my monarch, of myself too. I believe you Japanese understand that outlook. Have a care now for your own honour. You have committed an act of shame, an act that would not be approved by your Emperor."

Nishimura turned away and paced his bridge. There was truth in the Englishman's words . . . his act had been intended in his own interests, or at any rate in the interest of his cousin in Russian hands. The issue had now been forced and Japanese seamen would die, but not for *Nihon-koku Tenno,* the Emperor, Son of Heaven, fount of all honour . . .

Halfhyde said, "Make up your mind, Admiral." He paused, speaking deliberately though he was in an inner ferment of impatience. "There is something else. Leaving aside my torpedo-gunner's reaction to the use of your guns—he has orders to blow up your ship in fifteen minutes precisely from the time I boarded you, unless Captain Watkiss is produced safe and well. You have nine minutes left by the clock on the bulkhead. It's entirely up to you."

Vice-Admiral Nishimura glanced sideways at the clock fixed to the after bulkhead of his bridge. He swallowed, a gulping motion that made him look more toad-like than ever. He said, "Most wicked. Shall not surrender."

The seconds ticked away. The *Talisman* remained on station, her torpedo-tube covering the *Tsuyama* and Mr Stallybrass ready with his torpedomen at the firing lever.

When eight minutes were left Halfhyde said, "I suggest you bring Captain Watkiss to the bridge. There could perhaps be a compromise."

"What compromise?"

"More time for discussion. When Captain Watkiss reaches the bridge, I shall use your signal lamp to instruct my first lieutenant to hold his fire."

"Most considerate." There was a leer on Nishimura's face now, a look of self-satisfaction and approaching victory: the

Englishman lacked the guts of the Japanese. Nishimura gave an order and a seaman messenger left the bridge. The rest of them waited; a nervous wait. With three minutes to go, Captain Watkiss appeared on the bridge with an escort of two seamen. His face had a look of truculence.

"Well, Mr Halfhyde, at last! Have you managed to convince these buggers that I'm not to be trifled with?"

"Not quite, sir. Your pardon—kindly say nothing further at this stage." Halfhyde turned to Nishimura. "An Aldis, if you please —a signal lamp, on a long lead." He added, "Quickly. The time will soon be up."

A lamp was brought. Halfhyde, releasing the petty officer, took the lamp and moved across to the guardrail. He called the *Talisman* and was answered immediately. He flashed his message: *hold your fire and prepare to move in close.* Then he turned to Admiral Nishimura. "Your ship is safe for the moment," he said. "Now we will talk. You and I and Captain Watkiss. No others. Be kind enough to join me over here."

Nishimura gave a brief order. Watkiss's guard retreated; Nishimura beckoned Watkiss forward. Looking cross and bewildered, he came. Halfhyde looked down over the for'ard guardrail where his armed party still waited on the upper deck, formed up at the entry to the superstructure. "Gunner's mate!" he called.

Petty Officer Luke looked up. "Sir?"

"Follow my motions. No questions."

"Aye, aye, sir," Luke answered stolidly.

Halfhyde turned to Nishimura and Watkiss. "Now," he said. Then he moved like lightning. Seizing the vice-admiral's squat body, he lifted him and flung him towards the Japanese officers and men clustered on the port side of the bridge. Nishimura flew like a ball aimed at a row of ninepins. In the instant of maximum panic, Halfhyde grabbed Captain Watkiss and hoisted him with difficulty on to the guardrail. "Into the sea at once, sir, or you're a dead man."

"Damned if I'll—"

"You've done it before, you can do it again. For God's sake, sir, *jump!*"

With a terrified yell, Watkiss launched himself into space. He was followed closely by Halfhyde, then by the men of the boarding party, leaping from the main deck below. As a small waterspout indicated the submersion of Captain Watkiss, the *Talisman,* already on a closing course, came racing in at full power, rifles along her sides firing into the water ahead to deter the approach of sharks.

Bassinghorn's face was formidable. He said, "You went to sea without permission, Halfhyde. I don't deny that you were doing your duty as you saw it, but the Admiralty will regard that as no excuse. You realize that?"

"I do, sir."

"I shall do what I can to persuade them—"

"No, sir." Halfhyde was adamant. "It's on my own head, as I said to you not long ago. I stand responsible for my own actions. I am immensely sorry that things have turned out as they have."

"There were no further casualties?" Bassinghorn asked abruptly.

"None, sir. Only Captain Watkiss." Halfhyde stood like a statue in the commodore's day-cabin, blaming himself for foolhardiness, for going beyond all reason in his actions, trying to convince himself that some good had come of it all. Prince Gorsinski had been thwarted and the designs of his Czar turned aside: there was some credit in that. Likewise the Japanese had been shown that they could not with impunity challenge the British Fleet on the high seas. The Board of Admiralty would have to acknowledge a measure of success. But it would be dross to Halfhyde: Captain Watkiss had been his captain on several occasions and had had his good points. What had happened was tragedy; and there had been nothing to be done about it, no railing against the Japanese, no censure of nor attack with torpedoes upon Vice-Admiral Nishimura: the bullet had come positively from a British rifle, a sheer accident of aim. No blame was to be cast, other than upon Halfhyde himself for exceeding his orders and his authority. He had not even attempted to find out who had fired that fatal shot. It would not have been fair to do so. A sad business, and a sad return to port for all hands.

Bassinghorn paced his day-cabin, broodingly. Then he swung round and said, "I am going to tell you something in confidence, Halfhyde, just between the two of us. I did not tell you this when you joined my squadron. It was not germaine. Now I believe it is. I believe this because I have faith in you, and wish you well, and I know that you're suffering." He paused. "What I have to say is this: before I sailed from Devonport, almost a year ago now, I was told that Captain Watkiss was to remain on the half-pay list—although he himself did not know this, he was not to be employed again. He had become a liability in the view of Their Lordships—I shall say no more than that. But you know, as I do, that Captain Watkiss would have been far from happy with such a situation, one that would have led only to final retirement. That would have been death in itself for such an officer, Halfhyde. You'll agree, I know."

"Wholeheartedly, sir." To have been rejected by the Admiralty, by the British Fleet, would have broken Watkiss most cruelly. The sea had been his life; now he would be forever part of it.

Halfhyde felt an immense sadness nevertheless; whatever his peccadilloes and his often foul temper, Watkiss had been a patriot and a brave man and basically there had been something likeable about him.

Halfhyde listened to Bassinghorn's orders but scarcely heard them; he gathered he was to take the *Talisman* to Hong Kong, carrying Bassinghorn's own despatches, and upon arrival was to report to the commodore-in-charge. There would of course be a Court of Inquiry, which would be convened when Bassinghorn arrived with his slower ships. Once again, Bassinghorn said that he would do all that lay within his power to smooth matters. For the first time in his career Halfhyde was not fully in command of himself; in something of a daze he returned aboard his ship to give the orders for sea.